IN THE HOUSE OF BLUE LIGHTS

The Richard Sullivan Prize in Short Fiction

Editors
William O'Rourke and Valerie Sayers

1996, *Acid*, Edward Falco
1998, *In the House of Blue Lights*, Susan Neville

IN THE HOUSE OF BLUE LIGHTS

Susan Neville

UNIVERSITY OF NOTRE DAME PRESS
NOTRE DAME, INDIANA

Copyright 1998 by
University of Notre Dame Press
Notre Dame, IN 46556
All Rights Reserved
Manufactured in the United States of America

Design by Wendy McMillen and Jeannette Morgenroth
Set in 10.2/14 Nofret by The Book Page, Inc.
Printed in the U.S.A. by Thomson-Shore, Inc.

Library of Congress Cataloging-in-Publication Data

Nelville, Susan.
In the house of blue lights / Susan Neville.
p.   cm. – (Richard Sullivan prize in short fiction)
ISBN 0-268-01183-4 (cloth : alk. paper).
ISBN 0-268-01184-2 (pbk. : alk. paper).
I. Title.   II. Series.
PS3564.E8525I45   1998
813'.54–DC21   97-28953
CIP

∞ *The paper used in this publication meets the minimum requirements of the*
American National Standard for Information Sciences—Permanence of Paper
for Printed Library Materials, ANSI Z39.48-1984.

For John and Opal Schaefer

CONTENTS

Acknowledgments	ix
Abode	5
Blue	7
Your Own Most Quiet Voice	23
Eclipse	41
Hard Candy	57
On Love	67
Shaker	81
Witch	93
The Ice House Tavern	103
August	113
Quinella	125
The Increasing Distance	135
Night Train	155

ACKNOWLEDGMENTS

August, *Georgia Review*
Blue, *Crazyhorse*
Eclipse, *Mid-American Review*
Hard Candy, *Indiana Review*
The Ice House Tavern, *32 Pages*
The Increasing Distance, *32 Pages*
Night Train, *Sycamore Review*
On Love, *Notre Dame Review*
Shaker, *Indiana Review.* Reprinted in *Indiannual*
Witch, *Gulf Stream Magazine*
Your Own Most Quiet Voice, *Crazyhorse*

With thanks to Barbara Shoup, Kent Calder, Valerie Sayers, William O'Rourke, Dan Wakefield, Shirley Daniell, and Butler University. With thanks to my family for their support and love. And with gratitude for the work of the late William Lutholtz, whose book *Grand Dragon: D. C. Stephenson and the Klan in Indiana* I consulted often when writing "Night Train."

IN THE HOUSE OF BLUE LIGHTS

Questions . . . Questions, and suppositions.
And now they sit in front of us, the children,
At their desks, hands folded. And what can we
    teach them?
Imagination is a terrible gift. Cultivate it accurately.

STEVE ORLEN, from "Imagination"

ABODE

Heat tumbles through the walls of her house. Wires burn in the kitchen. Light blazes on the tile. The house smells of peat, of blackened wood, but no one notices. Every day she checks the house for fire.

Upstairs her children sleep, unencumbered. Upstairs her husband lies drunk from the weedy well. This is the husband who tinkers with lamps and clocks and wiring. This is the husband who puts the house to sleep each night and every morning wakes it.

They press against the night with four light walls. Its limits are their limits. Three times they've curdled blood into milk and held the cup out to the sleeping ones saying, Drink this. Drink this down.

Inside the house there is another house. The burning logs, the blue of smoke and flame. There's no way out, no visible way in. It lodges there, beneath the bone, its eight sharp corners wedged against her throat. She feeds the children sugared toast outside of it. She feels the boat of it against the brooding dock. It's where the other husband lives. The tumbling heat. Safecracker. Whether she is in or outside of the larger house, the smaller house moves with her.

All day long she checks the house for fire.

A woman who lives in two houses and calls it sweet and easy is a liar.

BLUE

My grandfather's second wife was raised in Florida, on the Gulf of Mexico, and every morning of her happy childhood, she woke to shades of blue.

Every memory she brought with her to her marriage was blue: the wash of color on her childhood walls and in her father's eyes and the eyes of the seagulls and the metallic glow of fish scales and particularly in the pale blue satin, worn and resewn, that bound the crib blanket she brought from home and kept underneath her pillow the years she and my grandfather were together, twisting that soft blue around the three middle fingers of her right hand as she fell asleep.

Sometimes the blue would pull away from the wool and then my grandfather would find her in the morning, tangled, with blue binding around her wrist or at times, dangerously, around her neck, all the sheets pulled from the corners of the bed. What do you do when you sleep? he would ask her. Or rather, he would say, while I sleep. Because he slept then, in the early years before children started climbing the fence at night, relentless as those showers of sparks you see falling in steel mills. He slept then the peaceful untroubled sleep of innocence or of the dead.

She couldn't say what happened while she slept. But as the blue became more twisted and torn, her sleep seemed to grow more fitful, and eventually my grandfather would catch her in the early evening with a needle and blue thread, patiently stitching the satin back onto the wool, always leaving an inch or two where she could insert the flesh of her fingers, the satin cradled each morning between her face and hand. When the binding was in place again, her sleep was more comfortable and in the morning she would wake with a sweet smile and she would make my grandfather coffee with thick cream and thick slices of bread with homemade jam.

Yes, he was jealous. His wife was beautiful and we never once in the years of their marriage saw her touch him like she touched that satin. When he tried to be tender she would lie silent and cold. In the day she was warm as firelight, but at night, he sometimes felt that he was entering an endless tunnel of unlit air, never the slightest flash of warmth or acknowledgment.

At night she could have been any woman, or not a woman at all, and sometimes, when he caught her hand creeping under the pillow where she kept the satin, knowing she would soon be pulling the ribbon of blue out of hiding to caress her own mouth as he lay beside her, he would grab her wrists and hold them away from the pillow, or he would take the hand and stroke it against his own face.

But she never touched him on her own like that, at least not willingly.

Some of this my grandfather told me. He was eccentric, and I suppose he thought that if he made it all seem understandable to me I would pass the story along to my friends, and they would tell their friends and so on. It makes sense, it's nothing, he hoped I'd say to every teenage boy in the city. She was an ordinary woman, not a ghost. He had no idea that as a ghost was to a boy, a boy was to me. I was terrified of them. He had no idea that I never mentioned I even knew the strange man who lived in the house of blue lights, let alone that he was my grandfather. It was part of growing up in my city to climb the iron fence to his house, looking for the ghost in the blue glass coffin or, eventually, the large white dog.

For a time my grandfather hired guards and posted them at the perimeter. But the teenagers kept coming. Some of them ran to the house and touched it. Some of them dumped stray cats over the fence. Some of them just told their girlfriends the stories, hoping it would have the desired effect. The purpose of ghost stories, my mother always said, is seduction.

My grandfather's office was on the sixth floor of a building still named for our family. The building is downtown, overlooking the memorials to war. This was between the two great wars of our century.

My grandfather knew the second war was coming from the day the first one ended. He never doubted it. When the second one ended, he began preparation for the third. That's why, when he died, there were all the drums of oil and bottles of aspirin and trays of nails and staples and the like arranged by size, like in a store. Over 30,000 people came to the estate sale. I was in college by then, and I remember the sale, all those people finally let inside the fences in the light of day, wanting to purchase something mysterious, uncanny, instead finding mason jars filled with paperclips and cans of peas and powdered milk. My grandfather loved his second wife. At the least, he could convince her that no matter what happened in the world outside, she would be cared for here in the gray center of the continent.

My grandfather ran our family's company during the first war. My father was too young to enlist, but he went to school and helped in the factory. The year the war ended, my father was sixteen.

Ours was one of the first companies in the nation to manufacture metal caskets in addition to wooden ones. There was a need for caskets during the wars, obviously, but even more a need for the parts of bombs they were able to convert some of the equipment into making. It was diversification, and the irony wasn't lost on my grandfather. The company served in the war as both the instrument of death and the cradle.

When the first war ended, my grandfather and father took the train to St. Petersburg, Florida, for a holiday. The trains were filled with men returning from Europe, and with reunited families. My real grandmother had died when my father was two years old.

It was during this holiday that my grandfather met his second wife. He fell immediately in love with her, and after a year had passed, he proposed to her by telegram and to his astonishment she accepted. A month later they were married. He brought his new wife back to Indiana. She was much younger than my grandfather, only four years older than his son. He of course convinced himself that the difference be-tween his age and his wife's was nothing and that the difference between his wife's age and his son's was vast. He told himself that she would be a good mother to his child. If at times, that first year, my father and grandfather's wife were mistaken for siblings, my grandfather didn't notice it.

It was January when he brought her here. She had accepted that on the maps of the world there were these green and brown places called continents floating in the cradle of blue, and that these continents had centers and that she would be living there and that, for the rest of her life, it would take her at least a full day, by train, to reach the ocean. She married my grandfather believing that their river would be blue. She pictured something like the Gulf, a warm vein in a landscape she'd seen only in photographs or paintings. She had never in her life seen snow. She pictured her married self as a blue-eyed princess living by blue water in a world of snow and ice. With a blue sky that stretched from east to west. Something like Antarctica or Alaska, only with sunshine and ice castles and white dresses and firelight in the winter and then three other sharply delineated seasons. She would have fur muffs and thick Russian caps and long coats lined with mink. The man she was marrying, she knew, was a wealthy man. She would have four separate closets full of clothes for each of the four seasons. As the foliage changed, the sky and river would remain, she thought, a constant blue, condensed and phosphorescent.

But you know how, when you head north toward the Great Lakes, somewhere in Tennessee or Kentucky you can see ahead of you, in the winter months, how the sky lowers its slab of gray and there's that line of opaque clouds like a wool blanket being pulled up over your head until you can't see anything outside of it? My grandfather's wife changed as they entered the northern gray, as though she'd entered some terrifying chamber. Like those enormous caves that begin underneath the ground in Kentucky become everything, all there is, an endlessly spiraling funnel. If only I could climb above it, she said, if only I could fly above the clouds. Flight had not become as it is now, commonplace and simple.

And the river. At its best, it was emerald green and at its worst, she said, a dull gray slate.

My grandfather told her that it wouldn't always be like this, but for the first four months of her life here it was interminable. Cloud upon cloud. She might as well, she said, have died. And there were the other clouds of smoke and filth from the factories, the coal dust, and the gray tree limbs and gray winter faces of their neighbors. She lost all color in her own face then, and you could see almost all the veins in her body, tiny blue threads. By April my grandfather was worried for her health. My father was in high school, and she waited each day for him to come home and tell her stories. Sometimes he had dances to go to, and ballgames, and my grandfather would come home to find her even more tired, and it occurred to him that she might never forgive him for taking her out of the ether of her childhood.

One day my grandfather called an engineer to his office. He had a plan. He would build a swimming pool. The engineer said that very few people built swimming pools in the Midwest. It was a waste of money, he said. There were plenty of lakes, and the amount of time the pool could be in use too small—only a few weeks every year. Build it like a basement, my grandfather said, and paint the inside blue. Make it the largest pool you've ever seen, as large as the pool at a hotel.

So they built the pool and lit it from underneath so it was this smoky chemical blue lozenge that you could see from every window at the back of their house. Blue as cura-

çao, as peacock blue ink. Their house was at the top of a
hill and you could see, in fact, a blue glow rise up from the
ground for miles, particularly on the horizon. The way that
shopping malls have that aura of pinkish-orange at night,
their house began to radiate that blue.

They started building the pool in May and by the end of
June it was finished and by July warm enough for my grandfather and his wife and my father to swim in the evening.
This is when the pool was most like that false iridescent blue
that I associate for some reason with test tubes, that blue that
has, in certain light, a tincture of yellow green, like that chartreuse that hovers within the red of Mercurochrome. In this
case it was a green that seemed to leech into the pool during
the day from the sycamore leaves that would fall on its surface. Every morning my grandfather's wife would skim the
leaves from the water where they floated like lily pads, like a
laying on of large green hands, larger than any leaf has a
right to be.

In the deep summer months that year, she seemed
happy. My grandfather would come home to bowls of fruit
and meat and cheeses and chocolate and pale pink wines.
Now and then she would find fish or shrimp at the market,
or crab legs that they would crack with their teeth or household pliers, dipping the sweet white meat in butter. During
the day, while he was at work, she and my father collected
things from the woods, and when my grandfather came
home, they showed him what they'd found. Stones and wild-
flowers and red and yellow mushrooms bright as traffic
cones. One week she found an abandoned hornet's nest as
large as a baby, and my father hung it from yarn in the
corner of the living room. On a good night they would all get
slightly drunk and swim underwater in the blue, my grand-

father's wife's long hair like a mermaid's, all of them lost in the giddiness of the pool. When they were in or near the pool, or when the moonlight was so bright it brought the reflection of the pool into the house, her face burned with a kind of fever, my father said, and she never turned away from them.

Then the children started arriving, and they had to build the black fence. It was the first generation of neighbor children to torment my grandfather. He had built, it seemed, a curiosity, and the myths began to grow around it. The boys would bring the girlfriends and sometimes my grandfather would hear them splashing in the summer months right outside their window, or he would see them hiding in the bushes or hear their footsteps in the fall in the dry leaves. He built the fence once and then again and then a third time, each time higher. My grandfather was a kind man, and if the children had asked to be shown around the yard, or if they'd asked to swim in the pool, he would have obliged. But not like this. Not hordes of boys running with their eyes all glazed and the girls squealing on the other side of the fence, the boys peering in the windows and doing cannonballs into the pool before running back to their friends.

As it was, it turned into a war of sorts, with my grandfather building iron gates and fences. Eight, then ten, then twelve feet high. The time that his wife was happy lasted only three short months each year, and because of that my grandfather felt he needed to preserve those months, to keep them for himself during the dark days, which by February each year began to seem, even to him, endless and suffocating. He looked forward to leaving the house during those months. The trip into the city, the bright lights on the desks, the whine of the saws, the smell of solder. He begged his wife to join a

Circle, even mentioned that she might keep the books in his office. There wasn't much for her to do around the house. She needed something, anything, to pass those long days between one June and another. She would shrug her shoulders and wrap her hair around the middle fingers of her right hand, and she would sigh and say she felt like she was in the middle of a mist she couldn't fight her way out of, that she wasn't fit company right then for man, she said, nor beast.

One year my grandfather enclosed the porch with thick glass. The glass had a purplish cast to it, and he added cobalt-colored lights and tried to grow blue orchids. The orchids died, but he kept the blue glass enclosure. That's when the white dog appeared, I'm told, a kind of husky, with eyes the color of glaciers. He came to the back door one night, and she took him in and he stayed, against my grandfather's wishes. The dog and my grandfather's wife would sit out on that porch in the late fall and the glass would drip with moisture from their mingled breathing.

My father went away to college shortly after the enclosure was built, and when he returned he was married to my mother and in a short time I was born. Out of the blue! my grandfather's wife said when she heard the news of my birth. Like that! she said, and she snapped her fingers in my grandfather's face.

One year, around Thanksgiving, my uncle bought thousands of Christmas lights, all cobalt blue. He came to my house and enlisted my father to help him string the trees with them.

My grandfather's house was surrounded by pines, and my father and grandfather wrapped branch after branch with blue lights. It wasn't enough. They went to every store they could find on the north side of the city, buying more. It took them one whole week to put them up, every evening and all day on two separate weekends.

The week before Christmas my grandfather bought his wife a blue silk dress with fifty buttons down the back and a sapphire necklace and bracelet and earrings and a blue felt hat with a veil and peacock feather and a blue velvet coat and gloves and shoes. And on Christmas Eve, after she opened the packages, he dressed her himself for church, fastening each one of the buttons over the satin of her slip, brushing her hair in front of the mirror, painting red lipstick on her mouth and rouge on her cheeks. Our church was a mile away from the house, in the frozen country, and the lights of their car caught deer and raccoon and squirrel in its path that night, and fat red cardinals in the ice-glazed sticks of trees that looked silver in the headlights.

The church was yellow with buttery light from the candles, and there was pine roping on all the pews with its thick scent, and red holly berries and the cobalt glass robe of Christ's mother in the window, and the sound of silver handbells. I was seven years old that Christmas, and I remember it. Before the first war, I was told, every mass in the church had been sung in German. Now the only remnant of the language was on Christmas Eve. *Stille nacht,* we sang every Christmas Eve at midnight as the ushers went from aisle to aisle passing their flame to our unlit candles. We raised our white flickering stars in the air. *Stille nacht.* Hitler's name was beginning to appear in the papers. I remember adults arguing about him. There were pictures of the beaming faces of children looking up at him, each face lit with fire. My grandfather was a businessman and had never trusted that kind of charisma. Every human being, he said, is a kind of wick waiting for light from somewhere. A merchant learns to take advantage of that, he said, as does a politician. The next war was hovering in the air like a zeppelin, and we somehow knew my father would be killed in it.

As we drove home that night my grandfather told us that so many Germans had located here because this place—these forests, this sky, these rivers—reminded them of home. My grandfather's wife looked out the window at the dark. Like the Black Forest, my uncle said. The White River, he said, is the color of the Rhine. Why did they come here then? I asked my grandfather. For money, he said. I could feel the warmth of my mother and father on both sides of me. My grandfather's wife turned to look at us. My father looked out the window, and my mother bent down to kiss my hair. I could smell her sweet smell.

On the way home, to celebrate Christ's birth, my grand-father poured the adults glasses of wine, white as diamonds. I got to sip some from my mother's glass, and he gave me a cookie thick with icing. He'd kept the bottle and the crystal and the cookies in the back seat of the car. He wanted the wine in his wife's blood when they arrived home. He was a businessman, a salesman, and he knew what he was doing, he told me years later. Maybe if he painted the landscape with enough romance she would forgive him for bringing her here.

My grandfather's wife was beautiful that night, more beautiful, it occurred to me with guilt, than my own mother. I was seven years old and every adult seemed ancient to me, but I could see that, just as I was a generation younger than my parents, my grandfather was a generation older than both my parents and his wife. I never could call her grand-mother.

My grandfather had hired a neighbor boy to light the lights. It was the first time they would be lit. We had known my father and grandfather were hanging lights, but had no idea of the number, or the color. It was like the pool. When we were within a half mile of the house we could see a shimmer of blue above the trees, and we could hear the sharp intake of breath from my grandfather's wife. *Himmelblau!* was all she said. The blue of heaven. When we turned down the long driveway to their house, even my grandfather was astonished by the enormity of what he'd done. *Wunderschöne himmelblau,* he said. Human beings can do this.

We got out of the car and walked across the frozen ground toward the house. Everything was glazed with ice, and then the thousands upon thousands of lights, the blue seeping into the hairline cracks in the ice so it was all as intricate as blue beads in a kaleidoscope or twilight refracted in beveled glass. It was more lights than had ever been gathered in one place in this part of the country. You felt that you could dive into the light and that it would support you.

We were all there together, in that blue. My father, my mother, my grandfather and his wife and me. The white dog was there then too, I'm sure of it. I remember touching his pale hair.

Already there were children's eyes looking out of the woods, girls leaning into their boyfriends' arms. Even I could feel it. All the next week cars pulled up along the road to stare at the house. Early in the evening there were families, and then the later it got, there were teenagers. As the lovers looked up at the lights and their car windows clouded over with steam, my grandfather's wife would stand by the window looking out, in the middle of her cloud of blue. A torn piece of satin from the blanket had become too frayed to sew back on, and she kept it in the pocket of her robe. While she stood there looking out, she twisted the satin around her fingers, and this look would come over her face in the blue glow. Darling, my grandfather would say, coming up behind her in the light. And she would soften into him, there in the middle of the house of blue lights, the teenage-eyes looking toward them.

The forest used to be filled with wolves, my grandfather would say then. He told her every story he could remember from childhood about the wolves, so hungry in the middle of winter, their long teeth.

The children called my grandfather's house the House of Blue Lights, and they began to weave their ghost stories around it. The door between the living and the dead seemed much more permeable then. Everything was haunted. It was a kind of sickness. All through the country there was a passion for séances. The priest said there was an increase in the need for exorcisms.

She's dead! The boys spread the rumor that winter, and it caught. That's a ghost in the House of Blue Lights, they said. During the day she rests in the enclosed porch in a blue glass coffin. You can see the mist of her spirit against the glass. Her husband made the coffin, they said, out of glass and grief. Her husband. My grandfather. There wasn't a thing we could do to dispel those rumors. And in fact my grandfather's wife grew more and more pale that winter, translucent, and she stopped going out of doors. Every day, it seemed, there was snow or gray sleet. She wouldn't let my grandfather remove the lights. In February they were still burning, bleak and low, and my grandfather became convinced his wife was mad and that he'd caused it. The day those lights come down, she said, is the day I die.

My grandfather gave her pills to help her sleep through the night, but the blanket was always in tatters in the morning. All night, he said, she moaned and tore at it. Sometimes she would call our house after midnight, and I would wake and see my father talking to her in the dark, on the downstairs phone. When he would see me standing on the stairs, he'd send me back to bed. I'd listen hard and would hear the door open and then shut, quietly, and I'd try to stay awake until my father came back in but sleep would wrap itself around me like my mother's arms.

Often that winter I would find my mother crying, and I'd ask her why. Love is harrowing, was all she'd say. Once I asked her what that meant, and she said love rakes the devils out of hiding.

By Ash Wednesday it had been, by my count, more than two months since we had seen the sky.

One day after school I went to the house to make my grandfather's wife a pot of tea. She hadn't bothered to dress since the middle of January. I would go there every day, I thought, and try to wake her. You needed lights on in the daylight in order to feel the slightest spark of warmth. We were all feeling it, even me, as young as I was. I thought of this good deed, in some hazy way, as a Lenten sacrifice, and I was thrilled by it.

When I went into the house that Wednesday, there were no lights on anywhere. The heat was turned down low. There was ice on the inside of the front door glass. I knocked and no one answered the door, so I opened it with my key, a large old-fashioned brass key that fit the lock. I had carried it in my coat pocket all day. It was cold now in my hand.

The upholstery in the front room was an indigo velvet, and there was an old hair wreath on the wall. The curtains were that same deep blue, heavy and rich. Nothing was moving in the room. It was too quiet in the house.

It's a haunted house, all the boys said at school, ghosts live there. Years later, when I was older and it was whispered that a girl had slept with some boy in our class, it would always be here, in a car on the road outside this door. I could hear my own heartbeat then and later, when I would hear those stories, the memory of my heartbeat would merge somehow with all the heartbeats of all the girls who were ever here. There was a boy I liked then, and the thought of him was always hovering around me like an aura. I couldn't speak to him, but I could feel him suddenly within and around me, as close as my own skin. I walked into the house shielded by the dream of him.

In the dining room there were dried weeds on the table and an apple cut in two and turning brown. I was wearing a blue wool coat, and I pulled it tighter around me. My grandfather's wife had started cooking German food with horrid names, and the house stunk of it.

My grandfather had built a glass block wall between the dining room and the blue glass porch. I could see his wife sitting on a chair on the other side of the wall.

The white dog sat on the floor in front of her, his head on her lap. The lids were down over his eyes. He was trembling with the cold. I was only seven years old, and this is all memory. I touched the cold key in my pocket, and my teeth ached like metal on a filling.

I was only seven years old, and this is what I remember seeing. An ordinary woman, a white dog, a blue glass room.

But the story wouldn't stay still in my mind.

Once a young girl went into the house and saw the ghost, I would say years later. It was Ash Wednesday. The ghost had yellow hair, like a princess in a fairytale. It was the same color as the girl's hair. The girl watched as the ghost reached up to the hornet's nest hanging above her head. The ghost crushed a piece of the gray nest in her hands. She rubbed the ash across the white dog's face. The girl knew it was a dog with glacier eyes, but as she watched, a boy's face appeared beneath the smudge of ashes, a man's face, a face not unlike her father's.

The girl ran back home then, and as she ran, the story hardened to glass. Bewitched! she told her friends. Bewitched! She told everyone she saw the story of the dog and the ghost. All those young boys jumping the fences, their faces pressed against the blue window. How they multiplied, before the war. How they were drawn to that blue.

When my grandfather's wife was a child she lived in Florida. The blue was a fragile membrane visible only in daylight, like the iridescent edge of a bubble. On one side of that fragile skin was endless space, on the other a dark ocean. My grandfather and his wife are long dead, my father, and my mother. It took me years to feel sorry for them. Love is harrowing, my mother said, and she was right. The earth is only an imaginary blue. It spins here in the darkness.

YOUR OWN MOST QUIET VOICE

This was my childhood home. New ranch houses rising out of seas of mud. The futile attempts at seeding, and later, a veneer of sod. There were two trees in every yard the size of large flowers, wrapped in white tape and held straight by wires and sections of garden hose. The air was thick with white dust from gravel driveways, and in the summer, lightning bugs bubbled up from the cornfields which surrounded us.

Our neighborhood was as isolated as a country town but without a center. We were too far away from the city to drive there with no reason, on a whim. There were not yet any malls, just a grocery and drugstore that you had to drive five minutes to. We had very little furniture, but what we had was new. We drank hard water from new wells. For our time and place we were not wealthy, and not poor. We were postwar families building lives away from the crumbling city and a shell-shocked world.

The fathers left early each day and came home late. We hardly ever saw them. On the weekends, they tended to the houses which had spent the week in slow, unmistakable disintegration. Weeds wanted to take over the yard, pipes wanted repairing, workshops and garages needed wiring, new shingles had come loose from the roofs. They spent their few minutes a day with the children, their cocktail time with the wives, but they were married to their jobs and to these houses which enclosed their families in safety and in isolation.

The mothers took late afternoon baths, their skin blue-white, their arms round and lovely as they dressed, their backs discreetly turned to the children who sat impatiently on the bed waiting for the ritual of sweet powder and lipstick to be over. The mothers would be ready when the fathers came home, their hair still damp at the roots from the baths, dinner magically ready five minutes after the husbands walked in the door, the husbands who fought battles while the women waited at home and made vows to live like this.

It was, for the most part, a world of women and children. My grandmother lived in our third bedroom, and the talk in my house was all of fabrics and patterns and needlework. Silver straight pins glinted from the carpet where my grandmother had dropped them. Evenings, while my father watched television, my mother and grandmother and I would sit in the breakfast room off the kitchen, my mother at the table knitting, my grandmother rocking and knitting, the glasses of pink lemonade and melting ice, the rhythmic yellow-green of the lightning bugs caught in the gray screen behind my grandmother's head. I sat on the floor knitting uneven rows, and when I dropped a stitch, my mother or my grandmother helped me weave it back before the entire piece unravelled in my hands. We went to church every Sunday, and I had been told I had an individual soul that would be saved quite painlessly by uttering a few words and continuing to attend a church, with the exception of vacations and bad weather, for the rest of my life. But those evenings as a very young girl when I sat in the breakfast room so comfortably tied to my mother and grandmother, I knew it was a lie. My soul was at least three persons deep, a pure clean liquid poured from one cup to another.

My grandmother's room, painted a deep green and filled with dark pictures and china angels and embroidery, was a different world from the rest of the house. Each object had a history. In the center of the room was her sewing machine embedded in a card table. The table was covered with cloth pinned to brown tissue paper. The plaid arm of one of my dresses shuffled together with the blue bodice of my mother's blouse; there were stacks of collars and cuffs and stiff facings. My grandmother made every stitch we wore, the card table vibrating on the wood floor. Often she would prick her finger on a needle as she worked, and we would find a dot of rusty blood on the collar of a blouse or near the hem of a skirt. Sometimes my mother or I would walk by where she'd been working and be caught by a thread which followed us from room to room, unwinding from a spool minutes behind, unnoticed until we would try to get in the car and leave, and feel it tugging at our skirts.

Sometimes, when the sun was shining too brightly and my eyes would ache from the white walls and the silver faucets, I would go in her dark room and pull the curtains and be soothed by the greens and dusty rose and the black sewing machine and the pictures of deep river shadows and women in dark rooms filled with the clutter of books and dishes and children.

It was of course darkness we had banished from our lives. Our rooms were filled with light. Before we moved from the city, we had gone to a city church. The windows there were dark jewel colors: dark blues in Mary's robe, the deep red of blood and the brown of Christ's hair. The carpet and cushions were burgundy, the walls mahogany, the ceiling miles high. I would meet my mother and father after Sunday school in the round choir room attached to the sanctuary where rows of black choir robes hung like dark angels.

The city home we had left was in a neighborhood populated with old people who called our house by the previous owner's name. The backyard was filled with hollyhocks and columbine instead of annuals. My room was richly layered with years of wallpaper. But we left that all behind.

My mother had another child and we needed my grandmother's bedroom. I don't remember the day she left, just that the house was quieter. Her voice was missing, but mostly that other sound, the sound of activity, the grinding whirr of the sewing machine biting through cloth. It was too quiet. Her room was painted white. It was like a frost had settled. I grew. The baby grew. My mother slept during the day. She was easily tired.

All of the mothers worked in the houses, and the yards were too big, the houses built just far enough apart, that it was difficult to see the other women easily, in the course of a day. My mother had time on her hands. On a good day we would have contributed enough laundry that, if she did things slowly and carefully enough, the wash would expand and fill up the time between when my father left in the morning and when we all came home at night.

There were other rituals. On Monday she would scrub her comb. Tuesday scrub her rings. Wednesday scrub between the tile in the bathroom and the kitchen, Thursday the cracks where the walls turn into the floor. She was not good at chatting on the phone about nothing. During dandelion season she might talk, over a fence, with a neighbor woman, planning strategies on how to eradicate the weeds, most of the plans involving husbands and long chartreuse tubes filled with poison.

My mother had a bridge club she went to once a month, and about twice a year someone in the neighborhood gave a coffee where the women sat politely, saying things which, it seemed to me then, had little or no relation to what they'd really been thinking. It was understood that there were no tragedies, no dark spaces, that things were always going well.

When I came home from school, I could tell sometimes that she had been crying from the loneliness. She seemed to live for the stories I would tell her, though maybe that's just how good she was at love. I went through periods where I pretended I was sick so I could stay home with her, or rather, I didn't pretend. It was real—the stomachache, the headache—and not real at the same time. But she was so pleased to have that nursing to do, to take her outside of her self. And it was comforting. My brother and I were my mother's vocation, and with us she was infinitely good: the cool washcloths which removed jelly from my brother's face or brought down my fevers (the hours of patient attention all mine, the soft hand on my forehead, cheese sandwiches and soup at odd hours, the TV set wheeled into my room, the sound of her breathing and humming as I fell asleep).

The store was dark but not cool, the walls covered with old beaded and brocade purses. Nothing in the world is hotter than brocade. It was summer, and we'd spent the day shopping. We'd bought nothing. Despite the mounds of coins which appeared on my father's dresser each evening as he emptied his pockets, evidence to me of our wealth, my mother was obsessed with poverty.

But lately she would say she felt something thick and gray coming toward her and she would drop my brother off at my grandmother's, and she and I would rush away from the gray to the lights of the stores, and people, and all around us the things that we could need: metal appliances with ribbons of light and glass vases and new towels and shimmering clothes. But we didn't buy, we just looked. And that day we ended up in a junk store. Fishing lures, plaster statues, old 78s, coarse gray carpet that smelled like dust, a blue horsehair couch, musty sheet music, "You'll Get By (With the Twinkle in Your Eye)," "Nestle in Your Daddy's Arms: a Foxtrot Lullaby." In the back of the store old crystal, china, a Danish plate; things got more fragile as they got closer to the old man without legs. There was a jeweler's glass in his eye. His face was evenly moist, waxy, as if the top layer of skin had partially melted. He wore a heavy tweed suit, the legs pinned back at the knees with safety pins.

My neck itched as I looked at him. I wished I could run out of there, but my mother wanted to buy a metal fan with heavy blades that would slice the air until it was cool. Lately it had been hot, so hot that the heat was all anyone talked about.

I sat on the horsehair couch, picked up a cool copper pitcher, and held it to my cheek. I ran my hand down my legs. I couldn't imagine what it must feel like. They say you can still feel a limb after it's gone. I wondered how much of your body you could lose and still be the same person. I wondered if that's what it felt like to be a ghost or to be in heaven, your flesh rotting, the sensations still there. I imagined the legless man without arms, without a trunk, without a head, still sitting there. I was eleven years old, and my body was most of who I was.

I watched as my mother went up to the legless man, saying polite things she'd picked up from listening to women speak to clerks in drugstores: hot enough for you, it's hard to complain about the heat after that long winter. My mother said things like this to people outside the family, ordinary things, and it always sounded rehearsed to me. She'd learned small talk like a foreign language, and she still didn't have the accent quite right, but no matter. Have you any fans? she asked. Her stomach was as round as a bubble. I put down the copper pitcher, looked at my own stomach and sucked in air. Outside, the wind was blowing, a dry windy heat. The window in the front of the store was dirty and wavering, like an old bottle. Any light that could get into the store skipped large dark spaces then was soaked into pieces of metal and into the glass circling the junk man's eye.

He pointed to the back of the store, and she moved through a door into a small room where there were six large fans and one small one. She plugged them into a wall socket, and the store began to sound like a tornado. I watched her plug in more fans. My mother came out to where I was sitting; rust was smeared on her hands and one thigh. Come see, she said. I walked back to the room, leaned into the doorway. The wind from the fans quickly dried the moisture on my face, and I felt chilled. My mother stood in front of the six fans and let them blow her blouse against her stomach. She pointed to three and said, Those are the cheapest. Stand in front of each one, she said then, and tell me which ones are coolest. I stood in front of each one in turn. That one's ugly, I said, pointing to an especially rusted black one. That's not the point, she said, how do they feel.

Close your eyes, she said. I closed my eyes and felt my mother's hands on my shoulders. She moved me through the small room, from one fan to the next. She said tell me when you feel coolest, and I nodded, wanting to please her. My mother's hands felt strong on my shoulders. The slightest touch, and I knew which direction to move. We're like Fred Astaire and Ginger Rogers, I said. My mother laughed. At eleven, I was a fan of old movies. When I was younger, I went through a year when I could, at any moment, become absolutely convinced that I was Shirley Temple. My mother loved to hear me sing. She had a talent for becoming interested in anything that interested me. I did a dip and a slide in front of one of the fans, absolutely unafraid of getting too close to one of the blades even in that temporary blindness because of the hand on my shoulder. "Holiday Inn," my mother said, recognizing in some clairvoyant way the song I was hearing in my head. I danced across the room and she followed, keeping up without dancing. I felt filled with helium, my mother the ballast that kept me tied comfortably to the ground. We moved, the air blowing like a smooth cloth across my skin, pale green stars on my eyelids, her skin the same texture as mine; as I grew older, her voice often, mysteriously, appeared in my throat. I can't tell where one stops and the next one begins, I said, and opened my eyes.

Try once more, she said, and I closed them. That one, I said, as I moved across the room. And this one and this one. We'll take those, my mother said. I helped her unplug the fans and the wind died down. I tried on old boxey hats while she inspected the frayed cords and decided they were safe. Then I helped her carry the fans. Up close, the legless man had dirty fingernails, brownish-red spots on the backs of his hands, a

spikey black hair growing out of a mole on his face. I looked
away from him and down at the thousands of watch parts
on his work table, complicated nests of springs and glass discs
and anonymous gold- and silver-tinted metal. All those parts
of watches spilled and tangled together made me think of
small animals run over by cars on the highway, and I shook
my head, hard, to get rid of the thought, but it stayed: the way
deer deflate like water balloons so quickly into nothing, the
blood and horrible pink insides of raccoons, and I perversely
imagined those things inside of me and inside of my mother
and that legless man, and I shook my head until I was almost dizzy, but the thoughts wouldn't go away. What are we,
I wanted to ask her, how fragile, and I pushed closer to my
mother's warm body and she absently stroked my hair as the
man counted out her change and slowly the thoughts began
to disappear, and watches and animals and people became
whole, understandable, indivisible things.

Outside in the clear air I said what a horrible place I
thought that was. You think so? she asked. It felt good to me,
she said. She stopped for a second to untangle a cord which
had come loose from the fan and was somehow twisted
around one ankle. I thought about the legless man and asked
my mother if there was a God. Of course there is, she said.
She stopped walking and turned to me, setting the fans down.
She seemed frightened. You feel Him in here, she said, and
she touched her throat. And here, she said, and she touched
my ears, you hear him speaking. Oh, I said. She turned back
around. She carried the fans to the station wagon, and she
put them in the back seat, careful not to rip the vinyl seat
covers. I've heard him, she said. God? I asked. I've heard him
speak in this deep voice, gruff, all magnified and sometimes
hard to understand, a father's voice.

We got in the front seat then and headed for home, the two large fans in the back, blades encased in wire skeletons, staring toward the front of the car like children.

My mother woke me up at dawn to tell me the world was going to end. Her face filled with an expression from the center out, like a television igniting.

The skin on her face was loose and moist as wet clay. She had stopped sleeping. I dressed and followed her to the living room. Under here, she said. We crawled underneath the ebony grand piano. I cracked my head on the blonde wood underneath. She asked God to save her children. Outside the window, the air was milky with heat and pollen.

When the world didn't end, we went for a drive. Put on your shoes, she told us. The world was full of crushed glass and metal and we didn't want anything to slow us down. We're going out now, she said. Hurry. I have to get dressed, I said, and I ran into my room, put on some jeans, a t-shirt. When I came back out, my mother was waiting at the door with her purse. My brother had on a pair of shoes and socks and his pajamas. He's young, she said, it's all right for young boys to go out in their pajamas. I'll take just a second, I said, and I shoved him toward his room and told him to get dressed, to hurry.

She drove too fast. God talk came from her mouth. She had been a housewife but was now a prophet. She picked up my grandmother and then drove us to all the scenes of her life—her homes, her favorite restaurants, the graves of her father and grandparents. She drove too fast. On that wild trip we ate lunch four or five times. She had us sing. *Row row row your boat*, she sang. *Life is but a dream.* She talked rapidly to everyone she met. I was sucked into the festival spirit, the endless hamburgers and the warm green summer air. I was too young to understand the importance of restaurant and flower and gravestone. This is me. This is what I like, what I think about, who I am.

Sunday morning. Our new church had large clear windows, the leaves of young oak trees blazing white with sun against the glass. The walls of the church were a pale, restful blue. My mother and father were in the choir. It was the first of June, and the minister wore a green shawl over his black robe. He said we were to rejoice; it meant we were entering ordinary times. At homes, lawns were thick and waiting to be mowed. There was almost too much glory. The congregation was tanned and sleepy. There were announcements, the droning of hymns, a sermon about taking life easy. During the last hymn my mother stood up and walked to the rippling blue-carpeted steps, a woman waiting at a river for baptism. She plunged and the church turned, my beautiful quiet dark-haired mother. Her eyes were glassy. She had a message from God. In a Protestant church in a suburb in twentieth-century America, where everyone knew that if God spoke at all it was in the changing of the seasons or in your own most quiet inner voice, my mother said she heard God shouting and calling her, and there was no one in the suburbs where we sat frozen on Sunday morning to piece it together when she spoke in tongues.

We went to the hospital during visiting hours. The elevator went up six flights and opened out on glossy linoleum and locked doors, the windows embedded with cross-hatched wire. My grandmother held a brown paper bag filled with slacks, a shirt, and cigarettes and matches. An orderly checked one bag and removed the matches. At the nurse's station was a lighter the shape and dull silver of a large gun.

It pointed out, toward the patients. The middle of the barrel was hot and red as live ash. There was a line of men and women in old clothes and pajamas lighting cigarettes. The air was bent with smoke. Women in fancy clothes sat around a table playing bridge. Their husbands had asked for divorces. My mother was not among them.

I looked around for her. We went to the room where we last saw her, and she wasn't there. I looked in the bathroom. There was no mirror, just a metal sheet that distorted your face when you looked in it. I felt faint, felt sick, touched my wavy face. I'd lost my mother and was up six stories high, and the ground was reeling. I was young and selfish and had my own problems. I wanted her home. I had no idea in the world what was wrong with her, had never talked to a doctor or anyone who might know what was causing this. I had to come up with my own theories. It was such hard work, this double life. We put on a pleasant face for the world and had no words to talk about any of this.

We went back to the nurse's station and asked, and an orderly took us to where she was behind four locked doors, six counting the two we'd already been through. Her hands were moving constantly, shaking, like a palsy. She wore a plastic band around her wrist, like a price tag.

There were four rooms around a central room with a table. Each of the four rooms was locked. There was a window with more of the wire in each door. It's the medicine, my father said, the lithium. They're giving her too much.

She came out and sat in a chair, leaned back and closed her eyes. Welcome to the inner sanctum, she said. The orderly laughed as though she'd made a joke. Neither my father nor I laughed. I resented the orderlies, the nurses, the way they seemed so relaxed around the patients, the way they treated the patients like children. They should be more sober, I thought, respectful in the face of tragedy.

We left through the locks, the nurses smiling at us so cheerfully that I wanted to kick them. I wanted to kick the bridge ladies too. But I hoped that by the time my mother was let out of the room she was in now that all of the old bridge ladies would have left and new ones who had no impression of her would be sitting around the table. They would see her, thinking she had just, like them, come in briefly from the outside. They would recognize that she was like them and ask her, please, to make a fourth so they could continue playing. She would quietly and demurely say yes. We would have her dressed in fashionable dress. They would be so impressed with her that after they were all out of there they would invite her to their country clubs to drink tea and play tennis, to have glasses of white wine in the late afternoon, which they paid for with a signature. Forever they would sit like this, friends around wrought-iron glass-topped tables. And when I thought about my mother I would picture her there, while I was at school or with friends, and I would be able to continue doing whatever it was that I was doing without guilt.

The air conditioning in the hospital was too cold and still. It made the bright sun and heat as we left seem unreal, our skin chilled like we were coated with ice. I could still see my mother's hands—wet, cold, independent of her body, flying like white birds coming toward me or resting for brief moments on her throat. Unconsciously, I put my hand up to my own throat and it scared me, that habit of my mother's appearing unwilled as though it were all a dark magic, and I was afraid that I would, by accident, discover the spell, that I would disappear into thin air without the aid of magician's tricks, of curtains and boxes, my body left filled with something that wasn't me, something so scrambled it was unrecognizable. I looked around at the street and trees and at my father and grandmother, and it occurred to me that if my mother could lose that thing which allowed you to say that this is my mother, this is Mary, that is Bob and not Jim, what guaranteed that the tree or bus right there would not, suddenly, turn to particles and disappear, what's to guarantee the road would not fall away, that the earth itself would not break orbit and fly. What held things together and allowed them to unravel and what, in light of all this fragility, was the soul. If the inner life, the soul, could scatter as simply as particles of matter, none of us was anything at all.

A warm, sunny kitchen. My grandmother's house. She put this lovely ladies lunch in front of me—chicken salad and melon balls, pink cloth napkins and clear glass plates. Rainbow sherbert for dessert.

I don't understand, she said, I guess I'll never understand.

Afterward, across her bed, a row of dresses, skirts and blouses. How do you do it? I asked her. Oh, she said, you see the dress in your mind somehow and your fingers cut it out, it's simple. Most of the time, she said, my mind just swims with plans for dresses. When I finish one, I start in on another. When I finish one meal, I begin to plan the next, and day by day my life grew under my fingers like a sweater. And all I've ever wanted is for my children to have a simple life like this.

Later, we walked around her yard. She stopped to pull up weeds I didn't even see. She had nothing good to say about cottonwoods or flowering crabs, those messy trees. She'd planted red maples, columbines, bleeding hearts, and roses. Things you can count on to come back the same, year after year.

A neighbor's garage was filled with complicated junk, thick webs of spider goo and dust stuck to the windows and the door, a wrecked car in the driveway. I was sure I saw the glitter of a trunk. Treasure! I'd love to go in there, I said, I'd love to see inside it.

In a place like that, she said, there couldn't be a thing worth retrieving, not a thing worth going after. It's dangerous in there, she said, you'd lose more than your way. There are knives, she said, and broken glass, and heavy boxes close to falling.

I wanted more than anything to run inside and run back out. She took my arm. Promise me, she said, you'll never go inside there.

My mother came home from the hospital, and we began a period of ordinary time. My father left work in the afternoon to pick her up, and he drove her to the back door of our house. He held her suitcase and opened the door for her. She was not completely well, he told us the night before, but you'll see that the worst part's over. She'd gained fifteen pounds, the muscles on her face were slack. My father put his arm on her shoulder and guided her in. My father was kind to her but formal. As though he were protecting himself from something. The first thing she did when she got in the house was put the paper sack on the desk and begin to take out things she'd made while in the hospital—two blue chess pieces with glazed drips hardened on the sides, some leatherwork, an unfinished collage made with bits of thread and twigs.

I'll make dinner, I heard my father say. My brother groaned behind him. Another casserole of cheese, catsup, and spaghetti. No, my mother said. I'll go to the store and do the shopping. I'll cook dinner. She jumped up from the couch to get a pencil. When she went into the kitchen, she had to pass where my father was standing in the doorway. They both tensed and looked in different directions. There was that formality that I supposed would take a while to leave. In fact, it never would leave. I wondered if they would talk at night about what happened, if we would all get together to talk about it, but even as I thought it I knew it would never happen. We would ignore it. I would never even mention it to my mother. And there were things—the hospital, the stories she told me—that I too wanted to forget about as soon as possible.

And thank goodness it was an illness she had gone through and come out of. Life was of course a moving forward. You were never in the same place twice. Suffering was supposed to make you grow, to make you wise. She had been through suffering and had come through and was now extremely wise. She had been through the suffering and was wise, and it would never happen to her again.

She'd be home a week before she removed the plastic bracelet.

In the ordinary times we learned to watch for signs. None of us, least of all my mother, could live completely easy. Was she sleeping, was she interested in God. Was she too busy, not busy enough. We noticed everything she did, became acute observers; the smallest tap of the cold cigarette on the edge of an ashtray could signal disintegration.

No one in our neighborhood mentioned it. She had disappeared, and she had come back. It would happen many times. And so it went on like this, in this childhood home.

Another family lives in that home now with their own tragedy, alone, unaware of ours, in the suburbs where people move in and out without taking root, in the suburbs which allow no history and where people keep their secrets.

My father has a new wife and lives in a motor home. He keeps it on the road. At night they play dominoes with Day-Glo dots. He sits at a picnic table, the awning hung with plastic Japanese lanterns, the night bright with color like a child's birthday. My mother and grandmother live uneasily together. My grandmother thinks by force of will and by her mothering she can keep the cloth that is my mother from tearing. So she sews my mother's clothes and hovers over her and reminds her to eat. When my father left, he blamed my mother's illness on my grandmother. Since he's gone, my grandmother has blamed it all on him.

And in the center of us all, my mother sleeps this drugged sleep, far away from the extremes of happiness and despair, in a low-grade misery and quiet courage that will have to do. Sometimes the red marks from the pillow stay on her cheek all day.

My grandmother and mother and I sit in the breakfast room off the kitchen of my mother's house. The shades are drawn. We drink bitter tea instead of lemonade. Tree toads have disappeared in silence from the face of the earth. There are fewer fireflies.

My grandmother is putting the hem in a dress for my mother. She is in constant motion. What are you thinking? she asks when my mother is quiet. What can I get you? she asks when my glass is empty. My mother puts her hand on her forehead. Are you all right? my grandmother asks. My mother gets up and goes in to the couch. Soon she falls asleep. Her feet as she sleeps on the couch are uncovered and round as a child's. An arm hides her face. Her legs are drawn up in a ball. She's touched the spindle, she'll sleep for one hundred years.

She has such pretty eyes, my grandmother says, such a nice figure; I've been trying to get her to wear a little eye-shadow.

The glass in my hand feels like a weapon. I've never felt like this. I go to the freezer for some ice. It wells up in me that this is, in fact, all my grandmother's fault. She has never let my mother go. My mother is only a too-obedient child. My anger swells and rises. It smashes windows. It floods the stars. I slam the door shut and turn around. Leave her alone, I am going to scream at her. Let her be.

There's a slight tremor in my grandmother's knotted hands. She is less than five feet tall. She is sewing a dress for her only child. My mother sleeps on. It would have been a comfort to find some human cause.

ECLIPSE

There was a tumor growing on his lover's left eye, on the white part, in the corner. It was slick and transparent, like scale on a plant leaf.

His wife's eyes were perfect, a rich brown. His lover's eye had had this mark as long as they'd been lovers. It wasn't fatal, but her vision was clouding over. As it grew, he'd noticed, she'd become less inclined to look at him directly, as though she were ashamed of it.

It's getting darker but not dark enough, his wife said from the lawn chair beside him; this isn't a total eclipse, is it. It was a Saturday morning in spring. Perfect weather. They were at their daughter's soccer game. They'd brought lawn chairs and set them out on the grass.

He told her no, it was an annular eclipse; there would be a ring of sun left like the black outline of the eye. He couldn't stop thinking about eyes. For the past two hours the daylight had been turning this weirdly mystical smoke color, like the world seen through sunglasses. It wouldn't happen here again, the paper said, for ninety-nine years. If he'd been someplace else right now, he could have missed it entirely; this was the best argument he knew for staying still. There will always be a moment when what you have aligns itself with what you desire. He'd read that someplace but didn't quite believe it.

He knew as many of the arguments for discipline as some medieval married man knew for the existence of God, and still he had a lover with a smokey film over her eye. He knew he was a greedy, shallow man, and he would apologize to God if he ever saw him, which he doubted.

In the paper, his wife said, they made it seem like such a big deal.

He could tell she was disappointed. He wished he could make it exciting for her. He'd always had this enthusiasm about stellar events. He was the only one in his neighborhood who'd actually stayed up all night watching a lunar eclipse. Even his kids thought that one was boring, nothing the least bit explosive, just glacially slow. They were more excited by meteor showers. Halley's Comet wasn't worth watching this particular century.

His wife reached for the eclipse-viewer. It was a piece of yellow paper with some kind of cloudy space-age film you could look directly at the sun through. Stars and moons stamped around the edges. Four dollars, and he'd bought two of them the week before. Four dollars apiece, and you could look under any tree and see the shadow of the eclipse through the leaves. Or hold one hand over the other with your fingers in a grid the way his son's friend was doing; the crescent shape of the sun reflected on the green grass.

Their son had the other viewer, so he and his wife shared. Their son, dressed for baseball, was sitting on the ground in front of them, watching the soccer game, now and then peering up at the sky through the lens. It was interesting, but more interesting to watch the weird light. The crescent-shaped shadow through the viewer was, in relation to the sun, somehow like a magic trick seen on television. Mysterious if you thought about it happening in front of you but somehow twice removed and so you don't quite believe that it's anything real, only trick cameras.

Feel my head, his wife told him and he put his hand on her hair. It was getting cold. You can tell there's a ghost in the air when you feel that kind of cold, he told her.

No, she said, you can tell there's a ghost in the air when you throw a sheet and something invisible holds it up.

How's Lynn's eye? she asked him then, and he flinched. He knew he flinched. The trick was to not think of her as his lover while he talked about Lynn, to think that he was talking about any woman.

The tumor grew back, he said.

Too bad, his wife said. I couldn't stand to have someone stick a needle in my eye.

Cross my heart and hope to die, he said, and then shouted instructions at his daughter. She wasn't playing her position. Good girl, he shouted, when she got back in line.

Kick it, his wife screamed, kick it hard. All the women screamed at their daughters like this.

Did you see those clips of Jackie O? he asked his wife. Jackie O was dying of cancer, and they were playing clips every night on the news. I realized I'd seen her picture everywhere but never once in my life heard her voice, he said.

Breathy, his wife said, like Marilyn Monroe.

All women must have talked like that back then, she said, our mothers too, I don't remember. All that power and she just lets out that tiny bit of air. And those boxy little linen dresses, and those little white gloves.

And everyone mourning, she said, over the loss of that kind of grace. I'd much rather watch little girls out there on the field, kicking the hell out of that ball. Can you imagine what kind of incredible women these girls will be?

JFK with his perfect hair, she said, and Marilyn singing Happy Birthday Mr. President with Jackie O sitting there smiling. They should have walked out of there hand in hand and left him sitting there alone with his presidential cake.

Do you think he was a bad president?

Reprehensible human being, his wife said, like Clinton. But that doesn't have a thing to do with what kind of president he was. I just don't want to hear about it anymore.

They stuck the needle in three times, right by the bone, he said.

There was a special filmy glass lens on the yellow eclipse-viewer that you could look through. He could see the image of his own eye reflected over the image of the sun with the moon taking a nick out of it. If he were his lover looking at this lens (and he often did that, put his lover in the scene he was actually living, like an overlay or scrim) the image of his (her) eye being eclipsed by the tumor would appear in exactly the same crescent shape as the sun being eclipsed by the moon. Exactly the same.

The needle went into the white of her eye, he told his wife, but entered through the skin surrounding it.

Thinking about the white globe made him think of her eye as an egg, the same texture as the white of a hard-boiled egg. It didn't matter. He loved everything about her body, loved thinking about it in different contexts, from different angles. Signs of dissolution made it all the more precious to him. She couldn't believe it didn't matter. She thought the fact that it didn't matter meant he really didn't see her. It's your own soul you're seeing, she'd say to him, your own soul rising up in front of you, not me.

She told him that when she was lying awake on the operating table, watching the surgeon cut at her eye with a scalpel wasn't at all bad. It was, she'd said, like lying at the bottom of a swimming pool, watching shapes and different colored lights just beyond the surface. If you didn't stop to think about what it really was, it was actually pretty. There was classical music on the radio, the distant chatter of the surgeons and the nurses, the hand and the knife never coming into any discernable focus. She told him she thought about him all through the surgery, rolodexing through the times and places they'd made love until she'd settled on the one she wanted to remember in detail.

Which one? he'd asked her. Sitting here now he remembered that he'd asked her, and that she'd told him. So he could remember her telling it.

He liked it when she talked to him, told him the story of what they'd done. She said she thought about it over and over during the surgery until the thought erased the place she was in the same way that thinking about her thinking about the story of it and how to tell him erased his wife, the game, his son slouching on the grass in front of him. He wondered what the surgeon was thinking about when he cut her eye, wondered if he wondered about the woman whose pupil was pulsing beneath his knife as she thought about her married lover.

He remembered the early morning steam when they stood by the window, even the grass was gray with it. Barges filled with coal heading from Cincinnati to Louisville. The fake

German facade on the motel. Their room was filled with antiques and reproductions of antiques. He couldn't tell the
difference between them, but there were little cards, explain-
ing which was which. They were crazy together. It wasn't real.
Before they checked into their room, there'd been a gold rope
across the door so tourists could peer in.

That was their first time. All the way to the motel, she'd
said, she told herself she wouldn't actually come, but there
she was. Tell me the story again, he'd say. He liked women to
talk during sex and he liked them to tell him the story of
what they'd done afterward. His wife used to talk like that,
but she'd gotten bored with it. The meaning had dropped out
of the words. For him, the words served as a lens that sharpened everything. Without that lens, he had always thought,
sex would be something else entirely. What that might be, he
could never imagine. That first time, his lover was so terrified
she couldn't speak. But it didn't matter. There was something
infinitely sweet about all of it. The overdone Victorian room,
the tourists periodically knocking at the door, the satin nightgown she'd brought to sleep in, her damp toothbrush, the
way her arm curved when she curled her hair, in the morning, with an iron.

I know I'm not the love of your life, she said to him, and
I came anyway. All I do is think about you, he said to her, I'm
crazy. You're crazy, she said.

Will she have surgery again? his wife asked him. All the
girls had come over to the sideline. It was halftime. Still getting darker. I can't get over my hair, his wife said. She had
him feel it again. Thick and dark and cold, even though it was
late spring, no clouds. Eerie, she said. Little kids were sitting
under the trees, rolling around in the crescent shadows. Eerie,
she said again.

I don't know, he said, truthfully. They've done it twice,
each time it grows back and leaves a worse scar. She's watch-

ing it I think. The doctor's watching her vision. He's given her
a million drops but some can cause cataracts, some glau-
coma, this and that. The more she goes to the doctor, the
worse it gets.

Typical, his wife said.

There was a ring of little girls surrounding a bowl of green
grapes, reaching in with their fists and stuffing them into
their mouths while the coach talked. The coach looked like a
parrot. The grapes glowed in the weird light from the eclipse.
He tried to think where he'd seen that color of green before. It
made him feel light-headed, oceanic, like they were all sinking
under in some endless tropical green water. His daughter's
team wore white shirts, and the more the sun was eclipsed
by the moon, the more phosphorescent the white became.
Eclipse light was pure somehow, the blues and reds blocked
off. He worked with scientists and they'd explained it to him
last week. Lynn's husband was, in fact, a scientist. They all
worked for the same company.

His wife went to the concession stand and stood talking
to one of their neighbors. As she walked back toward him, he
thought about how beautiful she was. More beautiful than
when he'd met her, more beautiful, if he were honest, than his
lover.

The game started again. His wife sat down beside him. It
was still getting darker.

Sam's having an affair, his wife said to him. That was the
husband of the woman she'd been talking to next to the concession stand.

Mary told you? He'd gone to their house a week ago,
with his daughter, to see if their daughter could play. It
was eleven o'clock on a Saturday morning. The drapes were
drawn, Mary answered the door in a white sleepshirt. He
could see the brown outline of her nipples under the shirt,
what he thought was the vague dark shadow of hair. The

inside of the house was gray and closed-in. He could feel cold air escaping through the front door like he was standing in front of an open refrigerator.

No, his wife said, she didn't tell me, but we both know I know.

He reached over and tangled his fingers with hers. He held their hands out over the grass and looked at the crescent shadows their fingers made. This is so weird, his wife said. It makes everything seem weird, I don't know. Shadows can look like fingernails, it makes you realize how weird everything is all the time. If things could be something else, it's weird that they are what they are. Like we could all be walking around with blue pyramids for heads or something.

Do you know how beautiful you are? he said. I watched you walking back over here to me, and you're still incredibly drop-dead gorgeous.

I'm getting old, she said to him. I look better in eclipse light.

You're not getting old, he said.

Everyone my age is getting old, she said. And so am I.

She touched her hair to feel it getting colder. The little girls on the field were dimming, running through a grayish-green light. The wind was blowing all the tree leaves.

You know, you don't need those glasses now, he said.

She took them off and turned to watch her daughter kick the ball down the field.

A week ago he'd walked with Lynn during their lunch break, and they'd passed a grove of horse chestnut trees in bloom. Loaded with thick red flowers. Look down in the blossoms, Lynn had said. They'd stood staring down into the flowers in the daylight. It was heady. There was a yellow line on the inner flesh of some. It was missing from others. The yellow line was there to draw in the bees, she told him. Sometimes walks with Lynn were like walks with a naturalist.

He'd driven by the house where she lived with her own husband and children. Her yard was filled with plants he didn't
know the names of. Plants with huge elephant shaped leaves
filled the shade under the trees; something was always in
bloom. He knew she was out there all the time on the weekends, in the evenings. She never covered her eyes. She was
sure that's where the tumor started.

He wanted to sleep with her in that house, sometime
in the daylight when no one was home, but she said she
wouldn't let him. Of course she'd said she wouldn't sleep
with him at all, and after a year he'd worn her down.

Once the blossoms are fertilized, she said, the yellow line
disappears. Like the reverse of the brown line that appears on
a human woman's belly when she's pregnant, like that.

The grove was thick and the branches hung down. He
put his hand on her breast, right over the shirt she was wearing. She pretended to squirm away, but he could see the way
her eyes softened and rolled, her shoulders relaxed. Not here,
she said. He threaded his fingers between the buttons, down
the swelling of her breast. He watched both nipples rise up
against the cloth. Not here, she said, and she finally pulled
away from him.

She moved out from under the shade of the tree. There
were fine silver threads where she parted her hair and fine
lines around her eyes. She wore sunglasses now, because of
the tumor, but he was walking beside her and he could see
the lines. He wanted to smooth them out with his finger.
He wanted to see her eyes. What if he did fall in love with
her? Maybe he was in love with her. What did that mean,
falling in love? Was there supposed to be something holy
about it? What did holy mean? The words, the concepts,
were as empty to him as space. They gave him the same
feeling he had when he left the house and was sure he'd left
the water running someplace but knew it was silly to run

back in and check. Just this vague unease that he'd forgotten something.

Do you ever feel guilty about this? she'd asked him then, and he told her he knew it was dangerous when he'd started it but couldn't say that he felt any guilt. Guilt was unnecessary. Do you? he asked her and she said that she did and he said that he was sorry.

She curved her dark hair behind her ears with her right hand. She was always doing that; it was this little girl mannerism. She dressed like a gypsy. She turned to look at him, but her eyes were hidden by the glasses. He saw his own reflection hovering in both lenses. Every day I tell myself I'm going to end this, she said, and just be married, or not be married, I don't know. Married, I guess. It doesn't matter who to, if he's kind. Raise my kids, plant my flowers, do my job, get old, and not worry about it.

Fine, he said.

But then I don't end it, she said. You call and I'm here. I can't stand thinking you'd find someone else. I know you would, and I couldn't stand it. I promised myself I wouldn't ever let myself get so crazy about you that it mattered, but I have, and it does.

He was supposed to say something then. He knew that. We both knew it was dangerous, he said again. He knew it was a lame thing to say. He could tell she was unhappy. He should say something else, but if he did he knew they'd enter into some crazy emotional quagmire that would feel like real pain but that, he knew, they'd both wake up from in a year or two realizing that it had all been just as much a dream as this was. He wasn't ready for that just yet, for their houses to darken, turn cold, he and Lynn with all the warmth in their own hands like burning coal. He wanted it to stay like this. It was perfect the way it was. Somehow eclipse light described

the place he was standing. Pure and white, but not glaring or
painful. Just fine. He never wanted to have to make a choice,
didn't see for one moment why he should. Why couldn't she
just float above this with him? There was no reason why any
of them should suffer.

They walked into the green glass lobby of the building where they worked. It was flooded with light and plants,
so she couldn't take her glasses off. The glass and the chrome
magnified the light until it was painful, even to him with
his normal eyes. There was the deafening sound of running
water in the copper pool in the center. Next door to their
office building there was a dark brick factory with green
painted windows where they made the pharmaceuticals that
he and Lynn and the hundreds of other human beings who
worked in this building decided how to make and sell. He
chose the color of the gelatin capsules that held the powders,
the color of the dye that went into the tablets. She wrote the
press releases. He was on the team that designed the look of
Prozac. She'd spent the last few years writing about it. That
was the project, he remembered, that had first drawn them
together. Sometimes he thought they should put it in the
water, like fluoride or some dense salt that would allow the
entire human race to float on top of all this useless pain.
At night, all over the world, people stood in front of their
medicine cabinets, opening amber-colored plastic bottles,
swallowing the pills because of his colors, her words, their
diseases, real or imagined. Even here, in the office building,
there was the stench of penicillin.

He said he'd get some money from the bank machine
before he went up. It was their custom to go up to their offices separately. They worked on the same floor. He watched
her go into the glass front elevator. He saw her take her
glasses off in the dark wooden tomb inside. He watched the

door close on her, was left staring at his own reflection. The mirrors were smoked. Even in the midst of all this light, he could see that he was fading.

There were tiny lights around the perimeter of the box, like in airplanes at night, like the lights in hospital hallways. Dark wood, soft music. An attempt to soothe. When the door opened on the yellow fluorescence of her floor and the potted plants, she didn't want to get off. She let the door close and pressed a button for the top floor. She would ride as long as she could. She leaned against the wall, her cheek on the cool dark wood.

She could hear the ropes and chains and pulleys or whatever it was that, hidden in the darkness of the shaft, made this box rise like some kind of magic. She wished it would keep rising, would rise and rise and rise and open on the moon.

When the door opened, she stepped out. Into the hall-way, a floor of mainframe computers and accountants in white shirts in their dull little offices with their dull little numbers and coffee cups that they rinsed each morning and wiped with brown paper to retard the growth of mold. The light here was as artificial as the light on her floor.

She walked down the hall to the metal door that led to a flight of stairs. The stairs ended in a room filled with sun-light.

The Museum of Medical History, and it was empty of human beings, as she knew it would be, as it always was, guarded by twenty stories and ashen accountants.

An entire building—two brick Victorian floors—that the company had plucked from the grounds of the state mental hospital when it closed and woven to the fabric of this build-ing, the lightning rod on the cupola like a witch's cap. It had been scheduled for demolition when the company rescued it

and moved it here, dismantled and rebuilt it with, as she re-
called, new bricks and plaster but the original design and
windows and all the insides just like they had been two hundred years ago. The scientists had meetings here once a year.
Now and then the museum was open to the public, retired
doctors drinking punch and eating sweet cake and talking
about snakeroot amid the pickled brains and rows of medical
textbooks.

She walked through the entry, through the old lecture
hall. There were torn black flaps of canvas covering the ceiling glass. A century before doctors had lectured here, cadav-
ers open on the wooden table. *This woman. This woman.* She
can see the doctor gesticulating as he spoke. *This man. This
woman. This body.*

Black electrical outlets. Cantilevered rows of desks circling
like a shell around the podium where the one person who
knew something in this room would stand and speak. A
doctor, and what did he really know? Nothing that mattered.
She didn't think that she herself would ever again know anything that she could say with any confidence.

She walked through the hall into a small laboratory.
Against the walls, oak cabinet after oak cabinet filled with
slides of human tissue a century old. She picked up a stereoscope and inserted fading Victorian pictures. Indiana farm
couples with matrimonial syphilis, the terrified expressions
on the innocent nineteenth-century faces. Thinking that in
their lives they lived outside the history of this place. Had she
ever been that innocent? Not in a long time. Had she always
been stupid? Extraordinarily so.

One hundred years ago researchers experimented with
giving syphilitic patients malaria to slow down the course of
the disease. She'd written about it in one of her news releases.

Now all these hundreds of men and women were here, their faces stamped on smoky paper, fine slices of their flesh stained and smeared on drawer after drawer after drawer of slides, the whole thing in this jaunty hat of a building plunked down on this modernist glass box. Drawer after drawer of human tragedy, and this is all it came to.

She sat down next to a row of microscopes, heavy black microscopes with clicking lenses that reflected green from chips of stained glass in the window. She thought of the clicking lenses in her doctor's office, the cracked-mud look of her blood vessels as the light shone into them and they hovered in the air in front of her, so real that she wanted to reach out to them, like a hologram of her eye, floating cracked clay, dried out soil, please don't let it be a question of love, it was too late for that, she can't let herself think of that. Two surgeries, three or four, and still the cells grew back and were starting to spread and, already, they'd spread too far to ever stop them. She couldn't tell him because she was afraid that if she did he wouldn't care. Her body was all she ever had to give him.

She was alone in this place and always would be. The women in the stereoscope were probably her age, but they looked old to her, and they looked, every one of them, like they were looking into a glare as intense and painful as the sun, a globe of burning light, and that was the last thing they saw, checking into the hospital so the doctors whose portraits hung on these walls could watch as their souls dissolved under the glare of disease. What was the soul if that could happen? An illusion, her lover would say. When all she wants is for him to tell her it's the thing I always recognize as you.

She was supposed to meet him Saturday, in the afternoon, after his daughter's soccer game. She had grown to

hate all of this. She wouldn't be there this time; he could wait
and wait for her.

There was a slide under the lens on one of the microscopes, ready for viewing. She leaned over it, her hand on
the cold metal of the barrel. It was like a gun. She cocked her
head to the left, to the right, trying to see something, to take
whatever was in there by surprise. Why was the metal so
cold in here, she wondered, cold as black wrought iron, cold
as window glass in winter, the condensation from her breath
like the streak of meteor light, a smear of cell.

She and her lover had gone to a planetarium together
to see Halley's Comet. But there was too much magenta haze
that night from the city. So the astronomer turned the telescope on the moon. It's spectacular, he said, the most unbelievable brightness. When he got down from the ladder he
described what he'd seen. She'd felt awkward as she climbed.
It was early in her love for him. And at the top, she saw it
too. An even more blinding white than he'd described; she
couldn't catch it directly, only in the peripheral vision. The
astronomer laughed when she told him. All night long people
have been making that mistake, he said; you think you're
seeing some celestial vision. What you saw in the glass, he
told them, was the reflection of your eye. Sometimes it's hard
to see anything outside of it.

HARD CANDY

I was sitting in the waiting room at the hospital, my mother's face above the sheets as dry as
winter grass. It was a cold night. We could hear
crashing all around as glazed branches snapped
off the hardwoods.

The moon through the window in my
mother's room was a chip of ice, the waiting
room littered with styrofoam cups. I wore my
coat and men's workclothes. I saw the newspaper
picture you had taken of the comet and I showed
it to a cousin.

It's nothing, he said, nothing but a black
empty square and a place in the middle where
the ink didn't take.

The cousins all sat there in cowboy hats. They
were effusive in their grief. They expected me to
give sympathy to them, and they never thought of

giving any to me. They were related by blood to my mother, and I was just some stray she'd taken in. They think of me as a hired girl, given room and board in exchange for boundless gratitude. Maybe it's my fault. I was supposed to become one of them. Something in my blood wouldn't let me.

So I came to see you. You might not remember. I wanted to do something unexpected. My cousins seemed like sleepwalkers to me. They stared a hole right through me when I said I was leaving. They couldn't have been colder. My mother was dying that night. You couldn't have known it.

The observatory was brightly lit. The entry was round, with marble floors, a ceiling four stories high, a crystal chandelier. It was ornate, like a funeral home. I walked across the stone floor to the open stairway against the wall and started up. I went up three flights and felt like I might not make the fourth one. The floor shone up at me, and it was polished rock.

A family with two rowdy children came running down the stairs. They were against the wall staying to the right, and so I had to move over they were coming so fast. I gripped the railing and stayed still while they hurried past, the kids shouting, one of them saying that he didn't see anything through the telescope, the mother telling him that he had seen Halley's Comet and he was to remember it to tell his grandchildren.

Big deal, one kid said, and the mother told them all to quiet down, there was too much of an echo.

I let them pass and then I moved back against the wall. Two women in their thirties, one of them holding a toddler, went around me. There was an odor of baby when they passed, that clean sweet sort of stink. I'm sure I saw it, the woman without the baby said. It was faint, but there.

They went around me without looking at me. The woman holding the baby moved back against the wall. That rickety ladder, I just wanted to come down, she said; I'm not even sure I looked in the eyepiece.

I stopped for a minute to catch my breath and to watch them descend. It was an older baby doing his best to fly from his mother's arms. The mother was looking at her friend as she walked. Once she almost tripped. I watched them until they made it to the ground, then kept climbing. Several other people passed me, every one of them disappointed.

It was like I was in line for the second showing of a bad movie, but I didn't care. I thought if I could only see the comet, things would be different for me. I'd driven by the planetarium many times but had never been in. I felt like I was taking a trip to a foreign country. I had high hopes, even though I knew I wasn't there at a good time. The comet would set soon, the best hour had passed, and this was the last of the good days. But I knew I wouldn't miss it. I would know that I had seen it. Maybe not to the naked eye, but in a telescope it would light up the sky with its fiery tail, a blazing whale swimming through heaven, a match heading for a wick, to set me on fire.

I came to the top of the stairs and went through a dark hallway. A cold breeze came from the other end. I walked through a door into an even darker room. In the center of the ceiling was a sliver of round frosted light, and it took me a moment to realize I was on the roof, under the dome, and was looking through a long porthole at the moon.

The telescope was larger than a man, long, made of black metal and mounted on something heavy and opaque. And you were there, just as I'd hoped. You stood, in a khaki jump suit, in front of a high desk covered with white star maps, looking into a green computer screen like an aquarium where words and numbers which meant nothing to me rose like fish.

In the center of the room was a rickety set of steps on wheels. A handful of people stood on them, a small woman on the top, squinting through a lens. I could see a bright reflection on the woman's watery eye. I joined the others in line.

The foot of the ladder was by the desk. You were looking through your maps, jumping up to answer questions. You thrilled at every one. Your movements were quick and light. You said you were a machinist, had worked as a cook and a clerk, that you were studying photography. This was the largest telescope in the country open to the general public, three times as large as any in the state. You used that phrase several times, general public. A year ago the dome was rusted through and leaky, the telescope broken. No one ever came here. You knew the comet was on its way. You wanted to see it. You were working at the university as a night custodian, taking classes in the day. Somehow, you talked them into putting a new roof on the observatory. You repaired the telescope. I had never heard you talk like this before.

You were the one who took the picture that was in the paper. You told us this was the largest telescope in the state. You mentioned this twice or more; you were so in love with the equipment, which you touched and coaxed and watched over like it was a child. It seemed as though it were sacred to you, to be the one who took the picture that would go in a drawer with the star maps for someone to pull out and marvel over seventy-six years down the road.

On your desk, you kept a blue tin full of hard candy.

Do you remember? We had a class together several years ago. You sat up near the front. You were excited about things, had talked to all sorts of people. You seemed wise to me. You

had a beautiful smile, beautiful eyes, beautiful pale hair. You
were so quick—your mind, the way you moved—like the
world was made of ice and all you had to do was glide. I felt
even more heavy around you, sluggish. You probably never
noticed me. I'm not one to talk voluntarily in class. Now and
then the teacher would put me on the spot. I would hear
slush come from my mouth, nothing that really mattered.

I was last in line. I looked over your shoulder at the
maps. Where's the comet? I asked.

Here, you said, and pointed to a black dot left of center.
You didn't turn around and look at me.

That doesn't really help, I said. I didn't mean to say that.
The map bore no relationship to the sky as I saw it, is what I
meant. Maybe it would all look different through the telescope. The maps were distinct black on distinct white. The
sky itself grew more muddy by the year.

It's true, you told me, you have to know how to read
them.

Maybe, I said. I took a piece of candy from the dish.

Help yourself, you said. I took two more and then, em-
barrassed, moved forward with the line.

You smelled clean when I was near you. Like sweet lico-
rice. You never turned from the computer.

As far as I could tell, I was the only person there alone.
Everyone else was part of a family, and they talked among
themselves. For a while I listened but I was able, finally, to
tune them out. Parents who bring their kids, late at night, out
to observatories, have kids who think they are the crowns
of creation. The parents nodded their heads with interest at
everything their children said. The families seemed bonded
together in a long, tightly linked line that led back to the beginning of time. Each set of parents held firmly in place by
their own parents. They were blessedly blinded by their chil-

dren. But I was never in the line. The bond hadn't taken. I was out there reeling.

I sucked on a cinnamon disc. The line stopped for a second. You swung around the room.

The center slice of the dome moved down, and the point of the telescope moved up. It was like looking down the barrel of a large gun at the stars. I hadn't looked at the sky this intensely since I was a child. It was too bad that without the telescope there was nothing to see.

Did I mention that I was in love with you?

When I was a child I saw a meteor shower. All of a sudden it was there, the whole sky, the way water balls and then streaks down cold windows as they warm, the way you moved around the room, all of it the same.

A woman in front of me was holding a baby. So many children in the world. The baby's head was small and red. The mother talked to a friend, but her mouth kept moving to the baby. She kissed his head and cheek, rocked gently as she stood. She did it without thinking. The baby's eyes were shut tight. The baby couldn't tell, I thought, the difference between herself and her mother, or the place where her mother stopped and the world began.

I wanted more than anything to be that baby, held like that.

Jeb, I whispered to you, quiet so no one would hear. Please look at me. I need to tell you about my father. He told me I wasn't any good. He came into my room at night. He gave me money and told me not to tell my mother. He went to church three times a week, and he spoke in tongues. He was sanctified and holy. When I was a baby and I cried, the family said my father walked me too much, afraid the neighbors would think he didn't know how to be a father. That spoiled me, they said. They said he should have walked me less.

I told you about his deer hunting. It's not that I'm like the
deer. I'm more the dark space that was there before the deer
and my father's lamp came together. (He should have walked
me more.)

My mother was always sick: her heart, the cancer, a general sadness that was always with her. I was supposed to
bind them together. I was supposed to make them happy. I
don't know how to do that.

And how can I explain this. My mother took me in
hoping for a mirror. And when I wasn't a mirror, she saw
nothing at all.

Last winter I went with her to visit the family in Kentucky. They lived back in the hills, not close to anything. We
went from one aunt's house to another. Each house had a
picture of the home place over the sofa, oil paintings done
from a photograph. The greens were always too bright, like
plastic easter grass. In each house a part of the family lived
out the winter all separate and closed in. Their walls were
dark panelled, the carpets red and dirty orange, the smell of
stale gas furnaces and old coffee. In every house there was a
tragedy, a cancer, a bad heart, a stillborn child. There was
always an old woman or a slow son staring out from a back
room.

My cousins spent every cent they could find or borrow.
We went out to the woods where one cousin was building a
house. The frame was up, the outside, the roof, but nothing
else. We walked through the fresh wood, the sawdust smell,
the discussion of windows and colors and doors. The cousin
so excited, a fresh start, a new house, a new beginning. In the
attic, the sun shone through the knotholes in the pine like red
stained glass. The cousin, her husband, their young children,
the new truck in the driveway, the aunts and uncles sending
money from their dark decaying houses, holding onto my
cousins in their brief flight upward. And as I stood in that

house, the shining faces of my cousins directing everything
to my mother, I knew it all. I could feel the house already
dust and filled with stale smells and the floor covered, the
windows shuttered, the closing in and my cousins' children
rising from the fresh decay and taking with them that picture
of the home place no one would ever think of offering me
because it is not mine.

So I came to the observatory to see the comet. I believed
in you. I hoped you would help me. I would look directly at
the comet, I wouldn't be afraid. I would learn all there was
to know in the world. Maps would seem real to me, chart-
ing something understandable. I would lighten, like you. You
would fall in love with me, my only hope.

I thought I'd wait until everyone left. I thought you had
to feel what I was feeling. The thick winter clothing I hide in,
if you would only touch me, I would do anything to make
that happen, anything for you to touch me.

There was one family left in line. A boy stood at the top
of the stairs, on his toes. I don't see anything, he said to you.

You looked at your computer screen. Then you ran by
me, so close. The ladder shook as you ran up it. You were accustomed to the height. You've got a great view of the fir tree
outside the window, you said. The comet had set, and the
telescope tracked it down.

Can we look at something else, the boy asked. You said
you'd show him the moon, a crater hundreds of miles wide.

When will the comet be back, the boy asked.

Seventy-six years, you answered. A whole lifetime.

The boy seemed unconcerned. He followed you back
down. I ran up the stairs and looked through the telescope.
All I saw was black. Can't you try and find it again, I said.
Please. I felt like crying. Maybe to the side of the tree, I said.
Maybe it's still above the horizon.

I'm sorry, you said. It's impossible.

It was the first and only time you ever looked at me. I doubt if you remember.

Hold on, you said, and you moved the stairs as I stood on them. I'm going to fall, I said; there's nothing to hold on to. I was up in the air in the middle of the dark sky, and the comet had come and gone and no one had really seen it.

The telescope swung around and pointed at the moon. Look now, you said.

The white glare from the lens hurt my eye. I had to move my head from side to side to see anything at all. I thought I might be blinking. What makes it disappear, I asked. You said something about a blind spot in the eye.

Once, when I moved my head, I thought I saw the comet in the dark place.

There's no fire in the moon, I said, not like the comet.

The comet's not fire either, you said, it's a chunk of ice that reflects the sun just like the moon reflects it.

I've seen the moon before, I said again, it's a useless, static thing. It doesn't matter.

I came down the stairs. You were lost in your maps. I tried to be witty; I can't remember what I said. I may have shoved against you as I left. I know you didn't notice me. My parents are unhappy. I suck on brittle candy. There has to be a reason I was born.

ON LOVE

They drove into town for dinner, to a fish place in an old house across from an engine factory. Fish breaded in cornmeal, deep fried, covered with hot mustard. Formica-topped tables with chrome on the edge, places where the pattern had bleached or worn off. Anna ate two bites of her sandwich. Both bites stuck in her throat. Lexey ate part of a tenderloin and a huge order of french fries with ketchup. Sam ate two sandwiches and kept Lexey entertained.

Anna looked out the window and played with her daughter's hair. She had no idea she was doing it, Sam thought, and he was fascinated. Lexey's hair was fine, honey-colored, and it reached to the middle of her back. It seemed to tangle easily. Anna's fingers worked the hair like a weaver with a skein of wool. She carded the knots from the hair then twisted it into a kind of pony tail, pushed the pony tail down through the hair into something like a french roll. Or she would take a section of the hair and braid it, rub the end of the braid against her skin like a paint brush, then let the braid sit there unfastened until it would slowly unwind with Lexey's motion. All the while she'd be looking out the window or over to someone sitting at another table. Now and then she'd stare at her daughter's hair, but not with a conscious thoughtful stare. She was someplace else, clearly.

It felt good to Anna to have another adult at the table, and the good she felt had nothing to do with adult conversation. It had always felt to her that a child rested in something like a hammock, that a child's feet weren't really ready to touch the ground for years and years. Or rather, maybe not to touch the ground, it felt to her that you never really touch the ground at all; what you had to learn to do was walk on nothing, on absolute and utter air. A child knows that in her bones; she could hear it in Lexey's night crying, in the way she clutched at her when she dropped her off at a babysitter's, in the ghoulish questions she would ask now and then about death—that the final thing a human being learns to do in this life is to walk on air. A child can't do that. A child rests in a ropey hammock, a web, and it requires at least two supports and should have more. She and the children live alone now, and only now and then she notices how exhausting it is to hold the hammock up herself; she notices it when there's someone else there to help hold it. With Sam around she can feel half of her body go limp, that constant watchfulness she's had since the children were born is eased with someone else at the table making sure Lexey isn't choking, telling her to get up in her chair when she slides down, as she just did, to pick something up off the dirty linoleum floor and

put it in her mouth, or she starts playing with the blinds on
the window next to their table, or when she cries because she
remembers Baby Jake is in the car and hungry.

On the way back to Sam's house, Lexey falls asleep with
Baby Jake in the middle of the front seat of the car. Her
thumb is in her mouth, her tongue is clicking, and the muscle
in her throat moves in and out like a gill. Her face and hair
are peach-colored from the sunset. Sam drives the long way,
out into the country. He loves to drive and he loves to talk.
He's been thinking about marriage. To anyone in particular?
Not in the particular, in general, about marriage, what it is,
what it means. His sister was married for twenty-seven years,
he says, she had three kids and the marriage was annulled by
the church. She was getting remarried in a month. He was
trying to understand it. His ideas of marriage and divorce got
somehow stuck in 1949, his sister had told him. I thought the
Catholic Church didn't believe in divorce, Anna said. She was
sorry once she said it. But it was relaxing to sit and talk like
this. He could get in a groove and go on for hours. Usually
she wasn't all that interested when he got into a Catholic
groove, like the time he was reading a book about the post-
partum Virgin. That was part of the same tributary of this
larger groove, she thinks. Divorce is wrong, he said, but not
annulment. God, she said, the Catholic Church, just change
the definition. She had never once in her life been religious,
though she liked to think that she might be forgiven for what
she was about to do.

You're a Protestant, he said; marriage isn't a sacrament to
you really, it's all abstract, you wouldn't understand. Some
sacrament, she said.

Lexey stirred in her sleep, and Anna brushed her hair
back from her eyes. She sweats in her sleep, she said. When

she was a little baby she'd have this sour smell sometimes, like rotten fruit, this adorable baby.

You can live with someone and not be married, he said, and have children with someone and not be married, and a priest can have you say vows when you're young, and if you choose to withhold yourself, or if you don't support one another fully, you haven't really married. Marriage is something that the couple does, and if it doesn't happen, then it's not really a marriage. The church is just acknowledging that marriage is a real union and not just some sort of legal contract. A divorce happens when you really have been married, and you get to a problem, and instead of working through it to a stronger place, you dissolve the marriage. My sister says she held back, never really married her husband. She's ashamed of it, ashamed of the pain she caused him, of the lying she did. She feels a lot of guilt now, a lot of grief. But she doesn't feel divorced. She never married him.

If that's the case, Anna said, I've never been married.

If that's the case, Sam said, I have been.

Don't tell me about it, Anna thought. Not now. Please. I've got all the pain I can stand right now. I don't want to take on anybody else's.

She put her head back on the warm seat. She let Sam's voice wash over her. Lexey asleep, his voice droning on, that was the hammock that supported her for this one minute in this day; for this one minute she didn't have to support herself. Anyway, she said lazily, I'm not a Protestant, I'm a skeptic.

Lonely life, he says. Wherever you go, you have only yourself to take with you.

Fat chance, she said, me and three others.

She looked down to where her daughter was sleeping on the seat, then she looked out the window. Fields of corn were going by, fences and trash, abandoned barns, ranch houses, and above it all the thick black wires lining the road. You couldn't look in a single direction without those wires snapping the sky into shards of broken glass. Aren't they supposed to be burying those things now? It's all supposed to be underground. She hates those vile wires, worse than billboards, those thick snaky wires of electricity and human voices.

They pass one of those concrete block houses that look like somebody built the basement on top of the ground and then forgot to build the house. There are no shutters, no gingerbread, no wood—everything cold and gray and stony as a tomb. She turns her head to look at it as they drive by. Sam's going on about his sister, how he thinks that maybe her marriage had hit the edge, and if they'd turned back into it, kept working at it, they might both have been stronger for it, like working within a discipline or living in one place—there's a deepening, he said, a polishing, like forming a ruby out of rough stone. That's what he thinks, but his sister thinks she was never married.

Anna thought that the sister was probably just doing what one chemical or hormone or another was telling her to do, and that everything else was just talking to fill up the time you had to kill before you died.

The yard behind the concrete house was filled with riding toys and plastic climbing cubes in crayon colors. There was a green swing set with rust at the joints and, beside that, a circle of clothes hanging from the line. A young mother, maybe very early twenties, sat twisting on a swing, her hair hanging down in front of her eyes. There was a baby in a mesh playpen. The woman moved like her husband's shirts on the clothes line, like the leaves on the cottonwood trees behind her. Anna imagined her in the spring, still in that same spot, the baby walking but the mother still there, twisting on that swing, the air so thick with cottonwood seeds that Anna could almost feel them in her lungs just thinking of it, a kind of asthma.

Sometimes I think I'm a crummy mother, she said to him, I don't know, just such a crummy mother.

You're a great mother, he said, you love those kids.

No I'm not, she said. You don't know me well enough.

So tell me, he said.

I can't, she said, I just can't.

Try, he said.

You'll see what a crummy person I am.

I know what a crummy person you are.

Lexey has these tantrums, completely irrational ones like children have—I don't want it to rain or something she can't control, and it escalates, it's the age she is, everything is me me, a few weeks ago she hit a little boy with a ball bat, not hard enough to hurt him, thank God, but she had a tantrum when I tried to send her to her room because she couldn't understand why she couldn't hit him if he was in her way, but he was in my *way* she kept screaming, he was in my way, and especially if there are neighborhood children in the house and they're all talking at once. I have my own problems now, things I'm thinking about, and maybe we're in a hurry to go someplace and I hear this shrill witchy voice come out of my mouth, like before we came here today. I can't say this, I don't know why I just can't say this, but Lexey's saying she wants to buy something and I'd just taken her out for breakfast and gotten Jake a new outfit a day or two before and I've been getting her juice every five minutes and following her around the house when she wants me to come look at something. I'll do this for hours, patient, patient, knowing she misses her father still and wanting to make it better, then suddenly I'll snap—Get in the car! I'll yell, for no real reason, she doesn't understand where it's coming from all of a sudden, Get in the car! And what I'm thinking is even worse, it's murderous, I'll be going over some knotty place in my thoughts and they're all talking, saying come here, come here. I figured it out once and when we're all at home someone is saying "Mom this" and "Mom that" every four seconds on an average and usually it's simultaneous—a tantrum over something at the same time that the oldest boy is obsessing over baseball cards (he walks around sometimes for hours with a Beckett price guide, saying look, Ruben Sierra is worth fifty cents with a bullet, and this Ryne Sandberg, do you think it's in mint or near-mint, there's this bend in the corner) it's all Bach, all simultaneous, and I'm thinking this is my one and only adult life I'm living and I can't think enough to get it straight and in my mind I'm screaming at them to get in the fucking fucking fucking fucking car. Sometimes I'm afraid I'll snap and really say it, or I'll hit them. I feel like a witch, such an unbelievable witch. Other mothers seem so patient.

Just like you, he laughs.

Then we're all doing something wrong, and I can't figure out what it is.

Sounds like you spend all your time protecting stuff from kids and kids from stuff.

And my own mother's not well; several times a day she calls me and just sighs and waits for me to entertain her with the story of my life, which is a dull dull dull dull story. Not one of her dreams has come true for her, not a single one of them, not even her dreams for me.

You're one of the most patient mothers I've ever seen, Sam said.

Then why don't I feel it, she said, why do I always feel so knotted up.

I don't know, he said, I couldn't tell you.

People say that, they say I'm a good mother, but I swear to God I'm not even halfway close to decent. I try to keep the house neat—this sounds so stupid, who the hell cares if the house is neat, I'm not neat myself, but I can't stand to live in complete chaos. I'll work for two hours sometimes on just the family room and as soon as I turn around there's a weeping peach on the couch, some kid's eaten half of it and left it there, and the floor looks like a trash basket—fifty-seven baseball cards and gum wrappers and bits of who knows what and always always the wrappers from Band-Aids and always always someone's crying and always always the boys and the apple cores behind the seat cushions. The way I tell the changing seasons has nothing to do with weather and everything to do with household trash. This season is peach pit and baseball card wrappers; next comes shriveled apples and school papers. I work all day and I come home and then the kids come home from school and all their friends start coming over, it's like I'm the after-school latch-key mom. And when I'm away from the kids, they're with me all the time like phantom limbs—there's no one in the world I love more—but since Mike left us I've had absolutely no white space, every minute we're awake together belongs to them, and I know I know I could say no, I want to read, go play, and no, I'm talking to a friend, go play, but it doesn't work. They stand there and they keep on talking, and with three of them, one is always in danger or always in a fight—last week a neighbor boy bit my son on the stomach the same day Lexey hit her friend with a baseball bat the same day I cleaned the house and they trashed it the same day another neighbor shot the garage door window with a b-b gun the same day Lexey's other little friend Allison was crying to go home because she missed her mother when I'd promised to babysit for two hours. My head is always spinning in circles, and I'm so exhausted, you have no idea how exhausted I am, and still I'm trying to please them—they're good kids, really, better than most—and I'm taking them to the zoo and to Mc-Donald's and buying them shoes, and really, I don't know how to explain this, they're not monster kids at all, they're adorable, absolutely sweet and wonderful and still I somehow am not cut out for this, I want a life, I want my own life, and I can't wait until they're gone to have it, I'll be too old, already some days I feel so ancient. Sometimes when I go to sleep at night my teeth are chattering I'm so tired, it has nothing to do with cold.

I'm sorry, Sam said. I can't imagine it.

I want someone with me again, she said. I want someone with me in my life, and how in the world can I expect a man to take on another man's children. It's hard enough, you know, when they're your own. Those days when you just want quiet, or when you're picking up after them and one of them leaps out of nowhere onto your back and screams, even if it's meant kindly, how can you keep, if they're not your own, from killing them.

She seems so sweet, Sam says, looking down at Lexey. Any man would love her.

I know, Anna said, that's why I'm convinced I'm such a witch.

That's life, Sam said.

I could spit in your face for saying that, she said to him.

She pulled her feet up onto the seat of the car, wrapped her arms around her knees. She was crying. He kept a box of opened Kleenex on the seat beside him; he'd moved it to the floor when they got in. He handed her one. It was yellow. He was such a bachelor. It seemed like a bachelor thing to her to be able to organize your life down to the open box of Kleenex in your car. She couldn't keep a box of Kleenex for more than twenty minutes. Her kids used toilet paper or paper towels or their hands.

It's just that you're such an introvert, Sam said.

After that tirade?

You've done that maybe twice since I've known you, he said, and it's always when you're tired or stressed about something or half-drunk. You've never been as much of an introvert with me, for some reason, but I've watched you with other people. Someone will ask you a question and there's no response for a while, your eyes move like you're reading, there's some dialogue going on inside your head and the other person sits there until you get what you want to say exactly right. I'll bet it's terrifying. I'm sure you didn't say half of what you were thinking just now, maybe not even a fourth. I'm usually the one who doesn't even know what I'm thinking until it's out in the air.

It felt so damn good, she said. But you're wrong. I'm not an introvert. I'm very open with people.

Like you're being open about why you came here.

To visit, she said, I've missed you.

I don't think so, he said.

He pulled the car over to the side of the road. There was an old abandoned house in front of them, a barn all gray and falling in upon itself, a rusted propane tank that looked as soft as suede. She had this overwhelming urge to get out of the car, to touch it. She could almost feel the splinters of metal in her hand.

Introverted parents are as good with kids as any other kind, he said. I'm sure it just feels like hell to the parents. You try to work everything out by yourself in your head while all around you there's this din of little people keeping you informed of every passing thought. It has to feel like jack-hammers sometimes.

You're right. It does.

You ought to join right in, let yourself be extroverted until their own little introverted genes kick in and you can all sit around being quiet together. They can be working out their adolescent problems at the same time you're working out your mid-life problems, which is how it's going to work you know, and on the surface you can all be smiling and polite until one of you explodes and no one has the least idea why because you haven't been allowed to watch it building.

If I said what I was thinking sometimes it would kill them, or something horrible would happen, the world would split in half.

Not likely, he said. It must be awful to think you have that much power.

I don't think I have any power at all.

They're both the same.

She went through a second Kleenex. They disintegrated in her hand. She stuffed the soggy mess into the pocket of her shorts and stretched her legs out so that her feet rested on the dash. He went on talking. She let him talk. She let him talk. He didn't know the half of what a miserable human being she was.

The car windows were open. She wished she could just let go, that she could let the world breathe for her, that it wasn't this constant conscious act for her. She had always been cautious. This is the first time in her life she had attempted to do something that wasn't cautious. She'd spent her life huddled against some sort of wall. She'd always been able to do exactly what she was supposed to do, supposed to in what she thought of as a very middle-class way. Whatever it was in her that developed the supposed-to fantasy was not the least bit creative. Supposed-to was nice, was sweet, was mother-wife-daughter.

She could do absolutely anything in the world that was expected of her only because the part of her that seemed to be really her was free to go its own way. She could think anything and keep the surface intact. She could be married to someone and in love with someone else or carry on a conversation about brands of children's shoes—honestly, she'd had long conversations about children's shoes—when she was really thinking about a lump in her breast or what the other woman was really thinking about as she talked. She'd done that her whole entire life, and suddenly, for some reason, she couldn't do it even one minute longer. It used to feel like freedom, but it didn't any longer. It felt like floating, disconnected to anything, and it made her angry. It was a force inside of her, something like a fire or, more accurately, a pressure. It was every bit as intense and real as muscle. She couldn't avoid it or turn away from it, she was afraid that something in her was trying to turn as transparent and hard as diamonds, and she felt out of control and terrified in the face of it. This is not how she was supposed to be. She didn't know how to mesh her vision of what a mother is, of how a mother acts and feels, with what was going on inside of her.

She was afraid that she was going crazy. She'd seen people go crazy, and she was afraid that that was what was happening to her. It was best, she thought, if the children didn't see. The children's father was impossible. There would be no help from him. Her brother could take the boys, but he didn't know what to do with the girl, he said, she was too young. Her brother would take the boys for a while and Sam would watch Lexey. He was kind, he loved children, he might be mad at first, but it would work out—and she would let herself go all-out full-stop crazy if that's what this thing inside of her wanted, if it wouldn't be satisfied until that had happened. She would go all-out crazy and then go back to her old self and never have to go through this again. Or she would go through this thing and come out of it an old woman and then she would die. Or she would go through this thing and then die without ever becoming an old woman, which is what she hoped would happen if it looked like this thing was going to persist. What did she want? What did she want from her life? She guessed that she wanted to sleep through it. She was strong enough, she thought, to handle whatever happened to her; it had never occurred to her before that she might have to make something happen. What she wanted from her life, she thought, was to become one of those wonderful calm old women—she'd only seen two or three of them in her entire life—but one of those old women who seem luminous, not happy necessarily, but luminous, like age had nothing at all to do with them and they didn't the hell care. It's like you could win or you could lose in your life and only rarely did a woman win and it had nothing to do with what happened to you or maybe even with what you did. It had everything to do with what you thought and felt.

There was a rusted-out trash can in front of the falling-down house. Back behind the house a car without wheels, all grown over with grasses and spiky weeds. We're not good enough for this place, she said to Sam, I know I'm not good enough.

It didn't disturb her in the least to think that some-day the whole universe would explode in a big fireball, that the fireball would consume paper clips and bumper cars and human hair and bittersweet and hawthorn trees and roses and all of Shakespeare without making one whit's worth of a distinction between any of them, that human beings wouldn't even be a flick of a memory in the mind of some non-existent god. It was what they all deserved.

There were bees all around the trash can. Yellow jackets. She could see them in the half-light. Everything had turned shades of blue with the sunset. Even Sam. Even her daughter's face. Everything but the bees, which were gold and flickering, like sparks of burning paper.

It was quiet in the car. The windows were open. One of the bees flew away from the hovering mass above the trash can and made its way for the car, through the open window in Anna's door, right for her daughter's hair. Anna was calm. She watched the bee fly and she watched it land as softly and gently as a moth on the tangled threads of Lexey's hair. And just as softly, just as gently, Anna, without disturbing Lexey, brushed the bee away with her hand. The cry that Anna made when the bee stung her and her finger started swelling was the softest cry of pain she had in her. Lexey didn't move, didn't make a sound, didn't drift even one level up and out of her deep and trusting sleep.

SHAKER

The ground was thick with wet, yellow leaves, the air gray with sleet. They felt like they were walking in a cloud. A part of a maple leaf tangled in his shoestring, another one stuck to the hem of her slacks.

They walked past a beagle sleeping in a pile of leaves. A cat watched them walk up the steep stone steps. At the top, the man stopped to pull the leaf off his shoes and the woman watched.

The lobby had white walls and was lit by electric candles. He went to check in and get their key. A yellow maple leaf loosened in the heat and fell from the leg of her pants while she waited. She picked it up and put it in an empty umbrella stand. Beside the stand was a wooden table with a stack of folders on it.

She ran her hand over the wood, thinking of the red in the grain. She waited for the oddity, the newness of a place she was not accustomed to, to settle from pieces (the glass candles, the wood floor, the pegs on the walls, the rag rug, waitresses in bonnets, the polished spiral stairs) into something that made sense. She held onto the side of the table until her husband came out of the office with a key and she saw that he was smiling.

Her purse was heavy and she carried it up high on her shoulder. He reached over to take it from her, but she shook her head and said, Men don't carry bags. He touched her hair and she handed him one of the folders and, even though she noticed his hand was trembling slightly when he took it, he was still smiling and shaking his head at some pleasantry the desk clerk had made and how he had answered, the whole encounter obviously successful.

They leaned into one another and looked at pictures of what they would see. A loom, she said, and they make brooms here. She took the folder and turned it over. On the back was a photograph of a sleigh in winter, another of people eating by candlelight, a third of people singing, all things which had happened recently in this place. She felt her sense of possibilities expanding so rapidly that she could feel the turning of the moon, the bright colors of the planets. She looked over at him, one side of his shirt collar outside the top of his jacket, his gray hair combed back. She took his arm and they headed back out the door, into the sleet. The cat followed them down the steps.

The first years of marriage they spent their holidays at home, the careful daily rhythm temporarily broken. Married people have hobbies, he had said. She painted eggshells, hanging them on a varnished leafless tree in the corner of their living room. She made hinged doors on some, and lined

them with velvet. He took up woodworking, going so far as
to make shutters by hand when she wanted some for their
bedroom windows. They learned to exchange small talk with
their neighbors.

Then after eight years, it occurred to her that other
people left their homes on vacations, that it was something
they could do. They started off with a trip to Chicago on the
train. She made a hamper of sandwiches and pop.

The first two days in Chicago were frightening—they
didn't know how to find a hotel, how to get a taxi, were
afraid they'd embarrass themselves ordering in a restaurant.
Their first hotel was a place with roaches. The third day they
moved to a nicer place where there were bellboys, ordered
steaks in a restaurant, and discovered Marshall Field's. They
spent half an hour trying on hats and bought some Frango
mints, and then ate them while he watched an inning of a
baseball game in the television department and she looked at
pillowcases and bought a bar of scented soap.

They were in Chicago for five days, and near the end the
burn on her chest began lightening.

The day before they were to leave, while she was ironing,
she had become frightened at the thought of going someplace
she had never been—the audacity!—and before she knew
what she was doing, pressed the hot iron to her skin. He had
heard her gasp and come running in from the porch, turned
off the iron, soaked a washcloth with cold water to place on
the burn, and taken her with him back to the porch to sit.

When they came back from Chicago, the old house
seemed new, as though it had changed dimensions while
they were gone. It took days for the walls to settle back into
their accustomed places.

And now they were here, the second vacation. Their
room was on the second floor of one of the outbuildings.

There were two sets of stairs leading to it, each wide enough for one person. It had the same white walls as the lobby, and deep blue woodwork, wooden floors, electric candles, a dim warmth and quiet. They settled in. He put his neatly folded shirts into a drawer, she took out a wrinkled dress and hung it on a peg. There were no closets. Except for the dress, she left everything in her suitcase and sat on the bed patiently while he put his things away—his hairbrush on top of the dresser, his comb next to it just like home. He went into the bathroom to put his toothbrush, toothpaste, and after-shave in the medicine cabinet. I forgot my toothbrush, she told him, can I use yours? No, he said, but a minute later changed his mind. She picked up his comb and ran it through her hair. He watched her, and when she set it down crooked, he laid it straight. Are you ready? she asked him and he said yes and handed her a ticket to the village. They both wrapped the string attached to one end of their tickets around a button on their coats. They had seen other people doing this. They walked out, the tickets flapping and turning against their chests like tea bags. He put his hands in his hip pockets and let her lead.

They spent the day exploring buildings, attaching themselves to tour groups and listening to talks. She became too easily excited, exclaiming over the trees, the people, checking her map, pointing things out to him. He trudged behind. By late afternoon, though neither one mentioned it, they both felt something rising up, something resurfacing that the rhythm of their other ordered life kept hidden. The leaves seem layered to her, like a pastry, or the wet layers of a child's papier-mâché. To him they seemed heavier, sodden, decayed.

When they went to the gift shop and she looked at handwoven place mats, he noticed a dead fly in the glass case. He thought of rusted overturned schoolbuses, rivers covered with film, beer bottles in fields, a row of old refrigerators turned face down in an alley near their house. For the first time in months he remembered, with terror, that some day he would die.

She noticed he was quiet and took his arm and slowed down for him and after they went through the weaver's house and then a shop where a man made a barrel, he noticed that she was talking nonstop about termites, from a show she had seen on television. The baby termites, she was saying, look, and I swear to this, they look like tiny glass puppies; they're absolutely transparent. Once a year all the babies are born with wings and they fly off, and when a male and a female meet, their wings immediately fall off and that's where they stay, I swear it. He looked down at her, squeezed her hand. He knew what she was trying to do.

They went back to their room and were ready for dinner by five, even though they weren't scheduled to eat until seven. She tried to take a nap, and he looked out the window while they waited. Dinner was served by quiet women in old-fashioned dresses. The lemon pie, she said to him, really is delicious. This is a good place, she said, a wonderful vacation. He noticed that her lip was unsteady as she drank her coffee, perspiration around her hair line. She had her hair set at a beauty parlor especially for this trip; the pants suit she was wearing she'd made weeks ago just to wear while eating this pie. Things like that broke his heart. She was having such a good time. Earlier he had decided to ask her if she minded cutting the trip short and leaving the next morning, but he decided not to.

These Shakers, she said, men couldn't be with women and women couldn't be with men, not even alone just to talk. But they danced in church.

She thought of how good it might be to have a place warmly lit to go to every night and be with people, and to be able among those people to turn if the spirit moved her, to scream if the spirit moved her, to stomp the floor and run and fall down among other people who were stomping and running and falling, chasing her hand out the door to who knows where in the wide world, the night and the day something she could move through freely, screaming with the joy she often felt but was afraid of. No one would ever tell her no, you don't feel the spirit move you; you need to be calm, to see things as they are, in the same dead way that we see them—it's not the spirit that moves you.

For a minute she wondered, while looking at her husband, a piece of lemon rind on the cuff of his shirt, whether her marriage had been a good idea. She wondered if maybe he didn't hold her back. I'm a balloon filled with helium, she thought, and he's solid rock. Maybe she was fooling herself that the quiet of their lives was good. Maybe they were half alive. Maybe there had never been anything wrong with her.

After all, she thought, this place, so beautiful, came from one woman so much like me. Mother Ann, she thought, I was born in the wrong time. No one believes in voices now. That afternoon, in the meeting house, she had read about Mother Ann, and she had sunk so deeply into her own private voice that she was afraid it filled the room, and she had snapped at her husband when he had come over behind her. She led him away from the place she was reading, wanting to keep it for herself. It made her remember. First things were bad and then she was reading the Bible and a voice in her would say maybe this is the explanation and she would see a spider in a window or a special color star and suddenly everything *meant* something, not a leaf or a blade of grass without a message, so it made her dizzy. She had learned, finally, not to trust the voices, but it made her feel strange now to think that someone else had gone through things she had gone through, and that this other woman had so much power, other people believing in her voices and creating this quirky lemon pie, this simple lovely chair. When she herself

had lost every job she'd ever had because of them. Her husband had been the only one to ever come close to believing in them, those first few weeks. He had been so quiet then, afraid of everything. She could talk nonstop, and he never interrupted her.

She looked over at him now, almost that same quiet. It would be so good to dance. She pictured the restaurant she had seen down by the river on the drive here; she could get in the car and go there, taking the turns quickly, dancing around the slippery roots of trees, sit at a table in a corner drinking coffee until her veins felt like hot wires.

She reached over to touch his arm. Let's go back to the room, she said. He stood up quietly. The cat met them outside. He picked it up and carried it. He would fight this, he thought, this time he would fight it. He put the cat down when he came to the door of their building. The cat tried to slip in between his feet, but he shut him out. He concentrated on the way the floor was made. He went up to a wall and felt the solidity of it. His wife was whistling, running up the stairs like a girl.

He thought of his own house, the overstuffed chairs with the small rips, the flowered slipcovers, the dusty egg tree, the endless things—would he have cream in his coffee? Would he have sugar? Would he have his car's oil checked? Would he go to sleep at nine or ten? All of this while fighting the feeling that none of it mattered anyway, the smiling gas station attendant standing on a planet where everything died, on soil that drank blood like bread soaks up broth. His wife turned back and looked at him, laughing as he started to follow her up the stairs.

Don't you remember, she said, the women use one set and the men the other. He stepped back down and went over to the other stairs and up to their room.

The next morning, after an early breakfast, she said she wanted to go to the meeting house a second time, and why didn't he go on to the woodworking shop. They could meet at the weavers and go back to the room for a nap before lunch. It was Monday, and the weekend crowd had left.

In the woodshop, he was the only visitor. An old man turning a chair rung talked to him about Shaker woodcraft as though it were really the nineteenth century, and he were a visitor having a conversation with one of the brothers.

He loved the smell of sawdust, the rusted tools. He told the old man about the shutters he had made, and the old man asked him if he would like to try the lathe. He said he would, and for the next hour he helped the old man with the chair. There was no ornamentation, nothing unnecessary. The old man hummed. Neither one felt the need to talk. He imagined how wonderful it would be to sit with one machine all day, hours of turning a wheel and pushing a pedal. On the wall in front of him was a poster with some of the old Shaker rules. Visitors enjoy them, the old man said; most of them laugh. *Always pray with the left thumb over the right. Never the right thumb over the left. Always kneel with the left knee first. Bedsteads should be painted green—comfortables should be of a modest color. It is contrary to order to have right and left shoes, to write a letter without retaining a copy, to leave a span of horses untied among the world.*

He remembered the last hospital. Awakened at six, breakfast in front of him, certain times for pills, for recreation. He felt tired from the ten-year effort, from trying to avoid it, trying to structure his life himself. It would be easier to let the inevitable happen, to relax into it, let things go sour. He wouldn't push it, just lose the energy to fight. Simple. *No unripe fruit should be eaten in its natural state. Blue and white thread should generally be used for marking. It is unnecessary to put more than two figures for a date.* This is a fine place, he said to the old man.

A good place for a vacation, the old man said. They began
work on another chair.

As she'd hoped, no one was in the meeting house.
Benches were pushed back against the walls, the center like a
ballroom.

She looked outside to see if anyone was coming. No one
was. At first she felt odd—all that space, and every sound
magnified. She could see her reflection on the floor. She began
moving. Yesterday, she had heard the songs. She had bought
a songbook. Soon she was stomping, running from one side
of the room to the other. *Who will bow and bend like a willow, who
will turn and twist and reel. O ho! I will have it. I will bow and bend to
get it. I'll be reeling, I'll be turning, twisting.*

The wooden floors shining with polish, wet yellow leaves
falling against all the windows. She had never felt this happy.
She whirled in the center of the room. Her skirt billowed. This
was where she'd always belonged; her life made sense here.
Her eggshell drawings were from the spirit. Nothing had ever
been as complicated as it seemed, not really. *O ho, I will have it. I
will bow and bend to get it.* She turned and twisted and whirled
until she collapsed onto a bench, laughing.

When she stopped laughing, the room was too quiet.
The leaves kept falling. The rain was turning to sleet. Something like fear bubbled in her throat. She reached for her
purse. Mother Ann spoke like this. *Vum vi-ve vum vi-ve vum vum
vo. Ve vum vi-ve vum vi-ve vum vum vo.* She ran from the meeting
house and back toward their room.

She saw him coming from the woodshop. She was coming loose, soaring. She needed to hold onto him. She waited
for him. He didn't say anything.

They walked into their building, the rag rugs, the soft
light on the walnut and cherry. A window by the door was
open, the windowsill wet. A maple leaf lay on the floor.

She headed up the stairs on the right, he the ones on the left. She looked over at him as they climbed, wondering if this were a joke, afraid somehow that it wasn't. *Believers should never use vulgar expressions like the following: I wish I was dead! I wish I could die! I wish I had never been born!* At the top of the stairs she got the key out of her purse and opened their door. He walked over to her and stood without saying anything.

One brother and one sister must not be together alone at any time. She went into the room and turned back to him. Hey, she said, wake up. Her face swam up close to his, but he didn't move. She turned into the room again, tried to think what to do. *Vum vi-ve vum vum vo.* She felt the danger in the moment, knew she should do the right thing but wasn't sure what that was. He had to come back or she would be lost. *Spirits do not move her and she cannot move him.* She looked out at him standing in the hall, the shoulders and the green jacket, the dear face, the hands, and she sat down on a chair, felt herself shaking. This is no vacation, she said, no kind of vacation.

The cat brushed by his legs and before they could stop he was in the room, a live yellow finch in his mouth. He held onto it gently with his teeth and the bird wasn't hurt, so they could hear the sound it was making. When the cat jumped and landed in the middle of the bed, he let the finch go. The cat and bird both screeching, the cat jumped from the bed to the dresser, the bird flying around the room and repeatedly into the window, and the loud cleansing scream came from the woman's throat. The man ran to her then, tried to calm her, opened the window and chased the bird outside, a flash of gold in the air, the cat out the door, the door and window both closed.

He went over to where she sat on the bed crying, and he put his arm around her.

For the rest of the day they sat on the bed and watched television. He filled a bucket with ice while she bought diet soda. They drank out of plastic cups. There were holes in the funny square ice and he slid one on her finger. She tried to put one on his nose. The ice glistened. One cube melted and made a dark wet space on the bedspread. Their arms and legs high up off the floor, they laughed like two children balancing a seesaw, at a park, in summer, in defiance of gravity.

WITCH

Her name was Julia. She moved here from the West. She came in one morning and sat at a booth near the back with a notebook that she wrote in. Now and then she'd look out the window or up at the tin ceiling and she'd grab a chunk of silver hair with her hand, and she'd twist it around her finger. If I was close, pouring coffee or cleaning plates, I could see the pupils of her eyes dilate so there was only this thin rim of blue like she had burned a hole in the sky and all that black empty space they say surrounds us had come pouring in and pooled.

We had no idea what she wrote in there. It was a hobby with us to try and sneak around behind her to look, but she was good at choosing a booth where her back was to the wall, or she'd close the book, slowly, as though she'd just paused to think, when we'd get near. Now and then one of us would come back to the kitchen with a phrase or a word we'd caught a glimpse of, and we'd sit around deciphering it as though it were something from the Bible.

Her hair was silver, but it occurs to me that I didn't think of her as old or aging, and aging terrifies me. I'd watched my mother's friends fade beneath their lipstick and their blush until the makeup seemed painted—same makeup they wore a year earlier, they were just not connected to it anymore, like a cake drawing away from the edge of a pan.

It got around that the witch was a writer, and we all tried to think of clever things to say around her so she'd overhear us. During a slow time, Randy the cook would come out from the kitchen and stand beside me, looking out the window, and he'd say something like "Damn squirrel last night, got in my attic and it took ten rounds before I shot him." He'd go on with some ridiculous story about stuffing bullet holes with bread and then his wife cooking the squirrel up in the pot, one of those glass brown pots, how he watched the squirrel's eyes bubble as he boiled. He'd look over to the table where Julia sat and she hadn't written a word, so he'd shrug and go back to the kitchen. But he'd be out again in a day or two with another outrageous story.

There were always animals in his stories, and violence. After a while, even the objects in his stories took on a personality—a gun that would never fire and a knife that, story after story, cut off heads so cleanly that they'd fall back onto the bodies, a thin line of blood beginning to ooze like a paper cut. After a while, I stopped listening to him talk.

Lydia, one of the other waitresses, got into the game too. She would motion me over to where Julia was sitting and she'd start whispering to me, but loud enough so Julia could hear, about her boyfriend. Her stories got racier and racier. He made her come in stranger and stranger places—abandoned

grain elevators and public swimming pools. If you could see
her telling these stories and holding a Pyrex coffee pot, leaning against the gold-flowered wallpaper, standing underneath
the barn prints in this place where everything's the same day
after day, you'd know how ridiculous it was.

I don't know how I knew, but I did, that it didn't matter
what we did or said outside of Julia. Maybe it was the way I
felt when I served her, that she didn't really see me. When
I asked her if she wanted more hot water and she said yes, I
never for one moment believed that it was me she was
saying yes to.

Julia was mine, I thought, she was no mystery to me. I
explained her away whenever anyone brought her up. Just
another crazy woman listening to her voices, I said, like the
old woman who collects Coke bottles and runs for mayor, or
the teenager with the red ponytail who walks around in a
dirty pink shirt and ducks under store awnings to sing and
then test the echo, a crazy woman, someone to feel sorry for.
She was childless. Her husband didn't pay any attention to
her. She was just crazy. End of story.

Myself, I have four kids, four of them. Every morning it's
chaos: four lunches to pack, no shoe ever staying with its
mate one whole night, morning milk spilled on homework,
stomachaches, headaches, loose teeth. Last week my kinder-
gartener walked into the kitchen with sanitary napkins glued
to the bottom of her feet so she could skate on the vinyl
floor. I start every morning patient, but they're sluggish in the
morning, oozing from one thing to the next in their own
sweet time as though the five minutes before the bus comes
is still enough time to get dressed, do homework, comb their
hair, look out the window for a while and stare, and before
they're all on the bus at least once every morning I hear this

shrill witchy voice come out of my mouth screaming at one or another of them to get moving.

Which is by way of saying that I have a full life outside of, in addition to, this place. I made it myself, willingly. Before I had my children I was afraid of death. It would come over me, now and then, like a shudder. After the first child, the fear began to fade. For years my life has felt like a place I built to hold out some dark ocean. A room, a clear white room. Somehow, lately, the witch has come inside. I'd like to be rid of her.

Then one day Randy knew more about Julia than I did. I went in the kitchen and he was there at the grill, painting butter on twelve slices of toast, scrambling eggs with a cleaver, melting orange cheese for an omelet. He was always moving, always keeping up a steady patter. I've got something to tell you, he said. No animals, I warned him. It's just a diary, he said.

She calls it a journal, but it's not a book she's working on straight through, he explained, just impressions. I asked him how he knew, and he said he'd met her one night at the Ice House Tavern. She was sitting in there writing, her husband off at some meeting, and he'd had a couple of drinks and gone up and simply asked her.

She just went in there? She just walked in and started writing? I don't know why that amazed me, but it did. It was something I would never do.

He flipped four eggs with a rapid click of the spatula and said it took some guts for a woman to go in there by herself and nurse one beer for hours, just looking around and writing down what she saw. She used to hate this place, he told me, and I asked why did she come here then, other places could as easily boil her water, and he said no, that he meant the whole place, the whole town, the entire Midwest, she couldn't stand it. She said that anyplace else in the world you'd walk down the street and even the store windows were exotic. She called us sleepwalkers. Even the churches are dull, she'd said, we don't really believe in anything.

He took the eggs and slipped them on two plates. I cut the buttered toast into triangles and put them on the side. I stuck a piece of parsley in the middle. The conversation made me anxious and then tired. I didn't like to think that there were other places to live your one and only life. You just hunkered down and lived it out where you began is what I'd always thought. I picked up the hard plate. I flicked the edge of it with my fingernail. It made a dull sound. I believed in things you could see. There was nothing else outside of that, nothing you could count on.

I delivered the eggs to two soapy old men in work shirts, sleep in the corners of their eyes. Three women, sincere in navy blue, had just come in from a funeral, and I took their orders. They gossiped about a widow who'd worn a fuschia shirt. Their mouths were bright with lipstick. I listened to the silverware, the sound of feet on the linoleum floor. I passed out mugs and ribbed plastic glasses, tightened the gritty silver lids on the sugars. Yesterday's pies had begun to bead and sweat. Fingerprints covered the stainless steel milk case.

This is just a rotting place, Randy said to me when I went back into the kitchen, a nothing place, a stalled car just rusting out and growing up weeds, and someday I'm going to fly away from it.

His hair was blonde and fine; it hung down in his eyes. He wore one dark earring, a cross or some kind of sword, I couldn't tell. His eyes were as blue as a bottle. I knew he thought his life hadn't started, that his real self was spinning its way along the highways to the coasts, testing the waters, beckoning him onto some wealth or glory. Spots of yellow egg yolk blossomed on his white shirt. At one time I was a little bit in love with Randy but would never tell him. That's another story, but I was afraid I'd flame out if I spent much time with him, just disappear. I was that crazy about him for a couple of weeks, but thank God some lamps that were glowing around him had switched off since then and he'd gone back to being the dark window he was when I first met him.

Sometimes, now, he frustrated me. I wanted to take him in my arms and teach him resignation.

So what else did you find out, I asked him. And he said she'd been a by-God vice-president of something, but she'd quit when her husband took this job, that she'd always wanted to write and decided she could do it here, that she could write about this place eventually since no one else had. And I said I'd set up a smoke screen if she asked me any questions. Like he did, I'd lie through my teeth.

She hears voices of dead people, she says she flies over town at night without her body, that she can look down at all of us and see the straight rows of our houses, the lights turned on and off. That's when I knew. A witch, I shuddered, and imagined her wild silver hair peering in my window as I watched TV with the kids or kissed my husband at the end of the day.

I think she's crazy, I said.

Not me, he said, I think she's great.

When she talks, I said, it's almost like she's foreign, or retarded. Even her vocabulary is odd, like something you'd hear in school but skewed, something not stuck to anything real. She says something and I want to look at her and help her start at the beginning. Egg, I want to say to her when she looks so thoughtfully at someone else's plate. That's an egg. Cup. Hot coffee. Toast. I want to brush so much melted butter on her bread that it would drip down on her hand, and she'd have to lick it or wipe it off. Butter, I would say. Hot. Greasy. Butter.

What else did you find out, I asked him, and he told me this story:

Julia and her husband had no children. After all the years in school, the years of nervous contraception, when they finally wanted them, it wouldn't take. Month after month they tried. They went to specialists. She got dye shot through her tubes, he jacked off into a cup. She told you this? I asked and Randy whipped a bowl of pancake batter and said, yes, she did.

It took five years, but when she finally did get pregnant, he said, she felt like a madonna.

I could see her, a silver-haired witchy madonna in maternity dresses that looked like bedspreads, levitating.

And this is the weird part, he said, bona fide flippy wonderful and deeply, deeply weird.

He poured the batter into Orphan Annie eyes on the grill. The cakes bubbled and looked up at me. He said she told him the baby was impossible. It was conceived, she thought, when it couldn't have been conceived, at the wrong time of the month, by two infertile people. When the baby was born, she planned to quit her job. Big bucks job, he said.

He flipped the cakes onto two round plates and I put them under the purple warmer. He poured bubbling soda water on the hissing grill.

But she was going to quit it. The baby would be a good baby, a quiet baby, and she would write a novel while it slept. It was coming because she needed it, this baby.

He scraped the breakfast grease off the grill and came over to stand beside me. I was drinking coffee. I held the warm cup with both hands.

It was a spirit baby, Randy said to me. He stood inches away. It was a spirit who chose to grow inside her body for a while, to grow a body of its own, to see what a body feels like.

No, I said. Come on. I moved away from him, poured myself some more caffeine.

Really, he said. He was whispering. A spirit, some sort of female ghost thing. I told you this was flippy.

I spilled a little coffee on my uniform. I could feel the warm liquid on my chest. If you were a spirit, why would you want to be a body, I asked, or rather, I asked what explanation Julia gave. And what did she say a spirit was, I asked, where did they live. And he said it was some sort of ancient energy thing, and that he thought it happened all the time in California. And something in me wanted to run from the kitchen, but I didn't.

Anyway, he said, the baby grew for seven months or so and then one day Julia started bleeding. She went to the office, bleeding, and for a day worked sitting down at the desk, putting on those pad things one after another.

Did she go to the hospital? I asked him.

First thing, he said, but the doctor said there was nothing he could do, that whatever was going to happen had already started. And since it was a spirit baby, she didn't worry, she thought it knew what it was doing.

The pain got worse throughout the day, and all day she was finding places to lie down, curled up in the restroom or hidden behind the file cabinet in her office, until a woman she worked with saw her through the glass in her door, and the woman called Julia's husband and drove her to meet him at the emergency room.

The baby was born an hour later in the midst of this white white room with all the chrome from the hospital ma-

chinery. And in the kitchen I could see it growing right there
in front of me as he talked, the whole scene: the baby born
and giving one scream before her heart stopped, the cord
wrapped around her neck like a slipped halo, the resident
freezing as the baby grew quiet, the nurse like a waitress
handing him the syringe, the epinephrine injected in the
baby's heart and the beat starting again in the baby's chest
but too late, the rhythm, too late. The baby's heart was beating, but she had fixed eyes.

And then, thank God, it stopped, the heart in that brain-
dead baby, and the gloves were taken off, and the aprons,
and the instruments washed, and the blood and slime rinsed
from the baby's body.

The end, I said.

But not the end, Randy told me, not the end.

He leaned back against the counter, his eyes bright blue
and waxy as a crayon.

In the room, he said, Julia could feel a glow like colored
fire, a joy, this pure ecstatic joy she felt, as though a spirit had
looked around for one minute with her fixed brain-dead
human eyes to see the world.

God, I whispered, what a world, a white sterile world she
went to all that trouble to see.

And I imagined seeing only this kitchen and later on, if I
was lucky, some desk, and I said that any spirit who comes
to life to see a hospital is a damn fool spirit and not worth
messing with.

But Randy went on about this mystical thing, this joy
thing as though he believed it, and he seemed suddenly so
naive to me, so much more trusting than I could ever be.
This is it, I wanted to say to him. It's all there is. The smell of
coffee and soap. Tables and chairs. The spatula in your hand.
It's all there is. Julia knew how difficult a child can be. There's

that constant sound of a child's voice interrupting your own thoughts and how much Julia seemed to value them, how she hated even the quiet hush of poured coffee when she worked. I wanted to go out and shake her, say liar, liar, witch liar. You were glad the baby died.

Sometimes lately, Randy said, she's felt her. The spirit has no voice to speak to her, no hands to comfort her, but she feels her in things, he said. Like what? for instance. He said she mentioned things like the wind that sucks the curtain to the window in her bedroom or in the sudden, papery clattering of leaves.

I felt this heaving sort of sob come up into my throat then, and he said they had the baby cremated the next day, that she carried the ashes in a smaller box until she could decide on the place to scatter them. At first she thought there wasn't a single place here—not a mountain or a river or a forest—worth burying the ashes of this spirit baby's flesh. Just the white rows of corn shocks and the red beans, she said, and the churches with their pews. But tonight, he said, we're going to scatter them. Where? I asked, and he looked at me and said maybe down by the creek, maybe under a streetlight, maybe inside the Dairy Queen. She's trusting, Randy said, in what the spirit tells her.

I went back out in the restaurant then. I filled ten glasses of water. I counted them.

After work I drew chalk squares on my driveway. I played hopscotch with my littlest girl. I held her warm body when she fell. Beyond the game the streets crossed as neatly as waffles. The mannequins in the store windows were dressed for the season. Dust covered the lamps in the lamp store window. Not a thing was out of place. Not a thing was out of place. Why did I have to hear this story? For days and days I've felt that baby in my arms.

THE ICE HOUSE TAVERN

The windows were open in the ice house, a big sliding door like a boxcar's in the back. The whole place felt cold when they walked up the wooden steps. An old man leaned out one of the brown brick windows and waved to the younger one. Hey Jesse, he said, hey there Jesse. He was one of those thin scrappy-looking old men, wild white hair and hazel eyes. Probably alcoholic, the girl thought, like roofers and house painters. Shrunk down by years and years of Colt 45.

It was late afternoon. The trees shone with a sticky sunlight. The air swarmed with cottonwood seeds, like ash from some fire you couldn't smell or see. You couldn't walk without getting them in your hair. The girl grabbed one from the air and rubbed it between her fingers. Slick as talcum and then that hard seed.

The girl was one of those young ones who serve you at restaurants, one of the sweet ones who's always at your elbow with water when you're thirsty. She was a girl you'd see on Saturdays at the Auto Parts, her uniform exchanged for her boyfriend's t-shirt, the t-shirt tied up high around her ribs. You'd see her walking languidly behind her boyfriend, following him as he maneuvered between green crushed glass wrecks, picking up car stereos with dripping wires or brooding in a dusty pole barn filled with dark, dismantled engines.

A week from today, she was marrying the boyfriend, the one she'd gone through school with. For months now, she'd barely eaten. She wanted to fit into the dress she was wearing to her wedding. Sometimes she'd look down at her body and like the way her belly circled in on the navel like a wheel. But more often, there seemed to be too much of it.

The man she was with on this trip for ice was not the boyfriend. He was a cook at the restaurant where she worked. Once a week he came here for a block of ice. He carved the ice for Sunday brunch. Next week she was getting married.

Hey Harry, the cook said, and they went inside the dark building and turned left, into the office where the old man sat, surrounded by yellowing papers and the smell of old coffee. The red light glowed on the coffeemaker, a record platter of burned liquid on the bottom of the pot. The girl walked across the room and shut it off for him. I'll make more, he said; it gets so damn cold in here.

The younger man sat in a chair and put his feet up on the cracked desk. Harry poured water in the top of the machine. There was a greenish film of old coffee on the white plastic lid.

The girl wandered around the office, looking at the framed black-and-white photos of Harry as a young man. In some of them he was pictured with a dark-haired girl. Divorced, he said when she asked him about the girl, years ago. She's remarried, he said, and you should see her house: all country frilly crap. I don't see how he can stand it, the new guy. Everything a woman touches turns goddamn precious pretty.

In among the family photos were pictures he'd taken, or cut from newspapers, of local disasters. The blimp that drifted away from the city and got tangled in the power lines, the deer that crashed through a filling station window. She heard gun shots outside, far off.

The old man asked the girl if she wanted coffee and she said no, just some water. He poured two cups of coffee and then filled a glass with water. He pulled a bottle out of a drawer and poured the liquor into his half-filled cup. He looked up at the cook who smiled and waved his hand, no, he was waiting until he and the girl went over to the Ice House Tavern later. The way the cook looked over at her when he said that. The way the old man smiled. He assumed they were lovers. She looked away from them. She was just here to see the place. It was, she'd heard, a place worth seeing. She was getting married in a week. The water in her glass swirled with white sediment.

The Ice House Tavern. That's why she'd come. You have to go there sometime, the cook had said. You can't live your life without going there. She'd seen it when they drove in. This old brown building like a railway depot on a model train. The drinks in that bar, he'd said, are crystal and unclouded. The ice slides from the house to the glasses without melting. There's never been a reported hangover; the liquor goes straight to your head and never makes you sick. And the ribs! God, he had said, the ribs. Straight from Adam. Sweet and red as blood.

All the time she'd worked with him he'd talked about the ribs and the unsuccessful times he had tried to duplicate the sauce. He'd finally given up when he realized he didn't really want to know it, that his weekly trip for ice would become a chore if he could make the ribs on his own any time he wanted.

When I eat them now, he said, I have to work to turn it off, that thing in me that wants to know the spice. So if you figure it out, he said, shaking his finger at her, if you have some sort of idiot savant culinary-mystical experience, please don't tell me.

She put the glass down and moved restlessly to the window, pressed a finger into the grime, pressed again, drug her nail in a line across the glass. She watched the cook drink coffee. He chewed the rim of the cup with his teeth. His thumb pushed in and almost crushed the foam. She felt like she was drowning.

The men drank the pot of coffee and she listened to the stories. Their voices droned on through tales of midnight hunting parties, out of season, for whitetail deer. Harry told stories about people pounding on his door in the middle of the night for more ice when they'd run out at parties. The things people do, he said, laughing, you wouldn't believe it, the things people do. I hear even more than bartenders, he said. If you go out for ice at three in the morning, you're falling down drunk and ready for confession.

It was as if they'd forgotten she was there, and she was listening in on the way men talk. They felt all of the sudden like a different species to her, their concerns and voices nothing at all like her own. She didn't know why that should be, but with a girlfriend she could laugh so hard it hurt, about anything. With a man there were bruised feelings, and the possibility, always, of misunderstanding or of being misunderstood. She and the boy she was supposed to marry would argue, and the next day she would remember only the closeness in the talking. But he would still be sulking over the meaning of some words she hadn't even known she'd said. And all the pizza boxes and empty cans of beer. How could they eat like that?

Her father was so loud, in the mornings, thumping down the stairs. A man couldn't be quiet if he tried.

A black ant crawled on the window ledge, another ant on his back or in his mouth. The old wood floor was warped and rolling as the sea. Outside the open window a breeze, a nodding of green so fresh that she could feel it on her teeth.

Inside, she watched the shadowy figures of men move large blocks of steaming ice with tongs and thick gloves, everything about the scene dark and muted and cold until they slid back the boxcar door and shoved the heavy blocks or bags of steaming ice out into the square of daylight.

She saw a man splitting a block of ice with a hammer and chisel, outlined in sunlight like he was made of neon, or an angel. The universe was a train, rushing faster than she'd ever known it to, a train doubling back and curving into its own open, hungry mouth. All her life she'd been hungry and she was afraid that it would never end.

I'm cold, she said.

Go on out to the car, the cook said to her, where it's warm. We're almost done. I still have to pack ice in the cooler, the old man said; then Jesse can come out and get you. He smiled at Jesse with an old man's lechery. Sometime, she thought, the two of them would be in here and she would be nothing more than a nameless girl in one of their stories. She stood up, and they laughed and waved her out into the sun.

She got in the back seat of the cook's car. She opened all four windows. The ice house steamed, and beside it, the tavern where she was going. Water, ice and steam. Nothing stayed the same here. The seat was warm. Catalpa trees in bloom outside the window. The smell of oranges. She saw white and then a fiery red. The car felt like it was rocking.

She was half asleep, half awake. A week from today, it would begin. She would be someone's wife. Night after night in the time like this she would lie in bed beside her husband's breathing body, his clean smell, his hard legs wrapped around her restless ones. But what if in the box of her head she would picture someone or something else outside of him? The cook, say, walking into the old barn behind his house, into a lean-to room where he kept his chain saw and his knives. The yellow lighted window and the clear dripping ice, the soft pulsing of his eye. What if she could hear the shrill whine of the chainsaw as it sliced the rough edges, or she could see the stance of his boots, the wet ice darkening his shirt. What if she could feel the glistening silver knife edge and the rough chisel and the cold ice on her tongue, or feel it under her hand? Maybe this other thing would be so real to her that it would balloon out of her head like an aneurism and burst into the room. She might turn toward the boy she had married and find something lying insubstantial there between them, and what then?

What would she fill her mind with, now that she was too old for dreaming. Grocery lists? Would she take up wallpaper or sewing? What would they possibly talk about, all those years they would be spending together. But he was a good boy, a handsome boy, there was no one better, she loved him. The church would be a field of dyed pink unfragrant daisies, of dotted swiss dresses like blown glass. Acres of clear blue windows, a cake iced with sugared flowers,

sweet gifts of towels and mixing bowls and ceramic dishes.
They would live together in a second-floor apartment. Her
parents had given them an old sofa and a plastic table. His
parents had given them a bed and two chairs. He would keep
his car out in the parking lot, it would become her car as
well, and on the weekends and evenings she would sit in a
lawn chair beside him, her legs drawn up underneath her,
drinking Cokes or beer.

Their hair would get wirey and thin, the spaces between
things they would say to each other growing larger and
larger like a reverse labor where the cervix contracts to hem
the baby in. In the dark, year after year, her husband would
move a long caged light on a wire from one side of the car to
another, and eventually one of them would die and then the
other. That's all she'd ever seen of marriage.

Oh, in between, they might have children. She would
call them Alicia, Jennifer, and Michael. Or Eyeshadow and
Cinnamon. She wanted to cry, she felt so sorry for those children. She imagined them sitting looking up at her with tragic
eyes and streaked faces. Always before, when she'd imagined
them, they were faceless. Well-brushed and obedient as dolls.

She hated that distance between what people said and
did and what they felt and thought. And now her own life,
like every adult life she'd ever seen, would be a tangled web
of trust and love.

She woke two hours later to the cook's face, his eyes, and
the smell of his skin buried in the jacket he was laying across
her arms. She moved her hips back against the seat to make
room for him to sit, but he just leaned in through the door.
He didn't seem to understand that she needed him. She
wanted to know if there was such a thing as love or what it
meant or how to recognize it. She wanted to know if it was a
thread you followed or one you cut, if it was something that

bound you to one place or took you someplace else. She was getting married in a week.

I'm dreaming, she said to him, I can't wake up. Come on out, he said, I'm hungry. I'm really not awake, she said; he said a little food will wake you.

The sun was so warm. She remembered a childhood vacation in Florida, a woman in a black wet suit emerging from the ocean and flopping like a huge shining fish onto the deck of a small sailboat. She remembered the colored beak of a toucan sticking through the bars of a cage and closing on her finger. There were no teeth, and the tongue was a long string of tiny hairs. She wanted to live like that forever. She wanted to stay a girl and see things like that. She never wanted to get married. She would find a way to sleep with the cook and tell her boyfriend. That would end it. She would keep ending and ending it, and she would never eat, and she would float above it like a spirit. Who said you couldn't do that.

Come on, he said, this way, and he led her over to the Ice House Tavern.

At first it seemed dark inside, and his pupils swelled and left just a thin rim of blue. Why can't you live without the brakes on, she wanted to ask him. Why does everyone seem to live their lives asleep.

They sat at a table by an open window. Outside, it was still full afternoon. Above the bar a sign: a white glass filled with ice, the name of the tavern in red script. Sticky varnish on the wood tables. Her eyes adjusted to the dark. Violet windows that melted and dripped in the sun like candles. A kitchen with a white enameled stove, a waiter emerging like a saint with plates of cake and slaw. Electric candles on the wall with scorched and tilted paper shades. Drunken shades. A pot of red bubbling sauce, the smell of crisp bones.

A strange sort of beetle, the size of a thumbnail and shaped like a leaf with legs and tentacles, a tiny green walking

shield, flew in the window and landed on his shirt. A crisp
white shirt with this beetle walking up the sleeve like he belonged there. This place felt good to her. There was a warm
groggy feeling to the room. She liked being in here with him.
Chips of sunlight sharp and cold as pins in the white curtains, across the dark tables, and on his face.

You like it here? he asked and she said she didn't ever
want to leave.

He said he would order for her. But food was unnecessary, she said. It hadn't meant a thing to her for weeks. It was
all tasteless as paste. When she thought of meat, she saw the
helpless eyes of the animal. When she thought of bread,
it clotted in her throat. I just live on love, she said, and she
laughed. She knew she wasn't wise. She wanted to move
through this world without causing harm. You know, she
said, I'm getting married in a week.

A waitress brought a slab of ribs and put the plate between them. The cook pulled one foot up on the chair, his leg
cocked like a wing, his head resting on his knees as he looked
at her. Let me tempt you, he said. The beetle's wings were a
fiery golden-green.

In the center of the table, a brass angel with a trumpet
in its pouting mouth, dangling over a white wax candle, the
angel spinning and dancing on shimmering corrugated heat.

Oh no, she said, you can't. I can't be tempted.

I won't let you leave here until you eat, he said. She
laughed and said, that's fine, it's what I'd hoped. He laughed
and said, now eat. She tested the sauce with the tip of her
finger, the way you'd test a baby's formula, a small taste to
see if it was too hot or too sweet. That's enough for me, she
said. She said I never want to leave here.

In the back she'd seen a windowless room with a twin
bed, a small table with a lamp, the kind of room you catch a
glimpse of in hospitals, near emergency rooms, where the

interns sleep on evening shifts. She would move into that room and never leave. The cook would come and go. She would live her life there.

When she could eat again, she would let him cook for her, she said. Princess food. Blind white fish that swim in the cold water caves of the Atlantic, the prehistoric insect ooze of shrimp. Small dark strawberries, sweet, the size of her thumb, fresh-picked, still warm. The sweet lip of meat inside the conch, that shell you hear the ocean in. The fresh snap sound of sun-warmed uncooked beans, the silky skin of apples, one grain of yellow rice, the juice of pears and peaches, the deep red stain of berries, the sting of pineapples. It would be enough. She would coat her bones with it.

She heard chickens cooking on a spit, fat hissing down into coals. Boiled in a pot of water, the flesh gets so soft it droops from the bone. When the sun warms ice-coated tree branches, the coating cracks and falls in a long slow single terrifying sheet. Why should I eat? she asked. It doesn't last. It never lasts.

Enough, the cook said, you have to stop this.

Marry him, he said. Just marry him.

AUGUST

We lived in that town for a summer. David found work at the veteran's hospital. I signed up for Manpower and worked when they called but had time on my hands. I hated it there. When I say it was a small town in Illinois, most people think trees and straight sidewalks and green lawns, but this was like the most congested part of an industrial city—broken glass, cracked sidewalks, chain link—with everything over three stories lopped off, the whole thing set in the middle of hot, dusty beanfields. The only green places were a park filled with trash and the hospital grounds. And there was a constant stream of veterans escaping, heading for the pavement, wandering in and out of bars in their pajamas. Every morning bartenders hosed down their floors while veterans watched, waiting for the waters to subside.

It's like I had died. Maybe it was lack of sleep. We rented half a one-story duplex, our bedroom window two feet away from the parking lot of an all-night Dairy Freeze. The night clerk was half deaf. They had 150 flavors of shakes. All night long we listened to teenagers in cars yelling shake orders and the clerk saying *what?* and the teenagers yelling their orders again. Sometimes I would lean out the window and join in, *Blackberry Shake,* he said, *Blackberry Shake, please give that boy a Blackberry Shake.*

David was able to sleep through it. I wasn't, though it probably would have been a sleepless summer anyway. David was five years older than me and ready for his life to start. But I was young and so confused about who or what I was supposed to be that everything was suspect, there only on trial until my real life would make itself blazingly clear to me.

I sat in the living room on muggy nights and watched the blue lights from the Dairy Freeze wash over the shiny cars and the girls leaning their heads on the boys' shoulders, their hair as satiny as the cars' finish. Somehow, my confusion centered on them, on those teenagers. I was only twenty-one, but I felt infinitely old. I had spent my girlhood dreaming about boys and nights spent in cars like that. If things were bad, there was always that escape. What else is there? You become an adult woman and your life stops dead in its tracks.

Mina lived in the other half of the duplex. She was one of those women who is so soft and inexact she seemed like bread dough that had risen too long and was about ready to fall back in upon itself. She was a woman of hobbies: crocheting dresses for bleach bottles, needlepointing covers for Kleenex boxes, cracking marbles in her oven and gluing them together into clusters of grapes. She was something to talk about while David and I made dinner on the old gas stove or

sat in the hot noisy steam of a laundromat, eating dusty peanuts from the machine at five cents a turn. She had lived in the duplex all her adult life, paying rent to an absentee owner who had turned the running of the place over to her. We lived with her tastes. Our walls were avocado, the kitchen marbled vinyl. Every table had two or three of her crafts on the top, including a giant bunch of the cracked-cats'-eye-marble fruit on a plastic veneered coffee table. We were in an unfamiliar place at the beginning of our lives, and she became the easy fabric of our conversation. When we felt separate, we brought up Mina.

She had this overwhelming impulse to make things—and everything she made, in the end, was ugly. It wasn't a matter of money. It wasn't from lack of talent. She could knit, crochet, sew, embroider, sculpt shapes. I thought she had just given up. I thought she was just killing time. She may have been young once, but that had died. She murdered every minute with sacks of glues and plastics and sequins. At night, I would see her sitting in the gray-green square of her living-room window, her hand holding a needle and pulling on a thread. And I felt this pull on my blood as if she were the moon and I the tide.

Then I met him. He was sitting on Mina's porch one afternoon when I came home from a temporary job. He was wearing loose green scrubs with a white tape that said V.A. over the shirt pocket and a splash of dried blood on the sleeve. His hair was blond, cut too short for the times, so I was afraid he was one of the veterans from the psych ward. Anyone who walked around town in scrubs was usually a serious escapee. I started back to the car but Mina came out and called my name. She was wearing a short-sleeved red-and-blue-striped tent dress, the flesh on the back of her arms billowing out. She ran up to me with a glass of lemonade in her hand and pulled at my arms, saying please, you have to come meet him, my nephew.

He was an orderly, the one who is supposed to smile and joke like an airline stewardess as he wheels you to anesthesia and the knife. He had worked his way up from maintenance because of his charm, Mina told me later; he made people forget they were heading into what was possibly the final sleep.

There was no family resemblance. At the time, I didn't think I'd ever seen a man as beautiful, although I realize now that by any objective standards, that if his picture were beside David's in a magazine, say, and women had to vote, David would win—I'm sure of it. But I fell in love with him in that teenage sort of way that lifted me up and made everything seem interesting and meaningful. I thought it was extraordinary. No one had ever told me that happens some-times when you're in love with someone else, that it will pass like bad weather if you let it. I sat there on Mina's porch drinking pink lemonade, enchanted by a flash of blue as a jay landed in the one tree in her yard, by a ruby hummingbird drinking from flowering tobacco, by all the sudden green in that town.

David came home while we all sat there, and Mina brought out more lemonade and worked needlepoint plastic canvas while we talked. Then I remembered that we had half a jug of cheap wine in the refrigerator, and I went and got it. The wine was garnet red, and we sat there on this falling-down porch on this glorious day with jewels in our hands, and we finished the wine even though it was a few days old and bitter.

The nephew got up finally and said he had to leave, and Mina said yes, she had things to do inside, and David

said yes, we were meeting some friends for dinner. The
nephew said he would be back again on Saturday because
he'd promised to take Mina garage saleing. Would we like
to go? David laughed and said he couldn't imagine anything worse. He had, in any case, to work that weekend, but
he said I'd probably like to go, and I said yes I would, and we
all went our separate ways. I was animated the rest of the
evening and before he went to sleep David said it had been
a wonderful day, and I agreed. And I fell asleep too, lulled instead of irritated by the flow of cars sailing past our window
through the blue watery light of the Dairy Freeze.

Saturday, there was just enough wind to keep it cool. The
nephew wore white deck shoes, without socks. Mina carried
an empty fishnet sack. I had a wallet full of silver money.
Doubloons, I said; we're pirates of the garage sales. Mina
laughed like a girl.

We went in the nephew's convertible, an old blue Buick
as big as three normal cars. We went from sale to sale. It
was clear that the nephew was not interested in buying, that
he was doing this as a favor for Mina. I was even more in
love. We would go onto someone's porch or into someone's
garage or basement, Mina cruising from table to table, asking
prices, picking up unmatched stained plastic dishes, china
angels with broken wings, electrical appliances with frayed
cords and narrow specialties (mushroom steamers, hotdog
broilers, bang curlers, birdsong simulators), and the thing
that seemed least promising at each sale, the least likely to
be useful or workable or attractive, was the thing she would
buy. She would leave, her fishnet full of some improbable
purchase, her face glowing as though she'd just netted the
most beautiful rainbow trout. And the nephew would listen
to her and respond with real enthusiasm. At each sale he
stood near the edge with infinite patience, no trace of bore-

dom. Now and then he would see something Mina would like, which he thought she had missed, and point it out to her. It was always the very thing she was looking for, Mina would say.

The first few sales everything looked like junk to me, but I walked around the tables, picking things up as though I were interested, afraid that otherwise I would seem to be there under false pretenses. And anyway, I was too nervous to stand near the nephew or to talk to him without Mina around. Up close I would have to make conversation, it would all have to seem real. At a distance I could be more aware of him, and at the same time more deeply imbedded in my own life, noticing the way the rough upholstery of two-dollar chairs felt on my skin as my arms brushed against them. At first all these things were props, nothing I would want to buy. Eventually, though, I saw things differently. I bought a cut-glass bud vase at one sale and carried it out like the Holy Grail. I held it on my lap in the car and it worked like a prism, spilling colors onto my hand and onto the seat cushions and the chrome on the dashboard. I leaned my head back against the seat, closed my eyes. I felt I'd been living in gray dead winter and been transported into the perfect blue of a travel poster. That's how good I felt.

From that one vase, the nephew knew what I liked. I became a collector of glass. I left each sale with something small and clear and fragile, something the nephew had pointed out. I became purposeful, the hours flew. At one house I stopped to look at a table full of mirrors, several of them lying flat and reflecting the sky like lakes. My hair fell forward onto the glass, I have never before or since felt that beautiful. The nephew's face rose up out of the mirror. Buy it, he said, and I did.

And so he stood at the edge of our saleing, subtly directing our movements, and it occurred to me that it was him; he

was the one behind so many of Mina's projects, those bas-
kets and sacks of things she brought home. They were under
tables at every sale, unfinished projects that everyone seemed
to have. He found them wherever they were hidden, and
Mina bought them for a nickel—the sweaters knitted and not
sewn together, or missing a sleeve, the half-finished afghans,
the needlepoint chair covers missing the background. Nothing anyone bought made the women sitting behind card
tables collecting money any happier, the weight of idle yarn
finally lifted, the possibility of a fresh start. Even I was sucked
in eventually, as I held an empty bottle of Joy in my hands
and felt the curve of a woman's waist. I turned to the nephew
and held a smooth rounded bar of pink soap, lifting it up to
my nose and breathing in the smell of it. It's a snapping turtle,
I said. I bought the soap and a box of pipe cleaners and
a dusty sack of marbles. And when we got back to the car, I
poured the marbles into my hand and let the sun warm
them, their wonderful hollow clacking sounds bringing some
childhood feeling back in ripe clusters.

It was getting dark when Mina asked the nephew to take
her to a friend's house. Her bag was full and she had grocery
sacks stuffed with things. He carried them up to the friend's
porch for her. Mina's friend came out carrying a bottle of
bourbon and two glasses on a tray, and the two women sat
on a glider with the tray on a table beside them. Before the
nephew was back in the car, their drinks were poured and
Mina was showing off her purchases, both of them talking
and swinging in the warm evening air.

So. I was alone with the nephew in a convertible on a
summer night, David working late. I was still a girl. I shifted
position. Closer to him? Farther? I can't remember, just that
the seat was still warm from the sun. We talked about the
car, about Mina, about the town. We laughed easily. I paid attention to every word he said. He listened to everything I

said. On the seat between us were all my purchases, the glass wrapped in newspaper. He wondered if I wanted to get something to eat. I said I did. He headed downtown and pulled into a littered parking lot behind some old buildings. He locked my things in the trunk. I followed him into a bar I'd always before been afraid to even drive by. It was the first time I'd been in a bar when the sun had not quite set. It was all dusky yellow light, just a few people sitting around at tables. There was one table of men in pajamas. The nephew seemed to know them, and I felt wonderfully sinful, deliciously sinful that there were people seeing us there together in the kind of place where nothing you do matters, a place I had thought closed off to me.

We drank. I think I drank more than he did. I told him about a movie I'd seen on TV the night before. It was a plot I'd seen every year of my life in one form or another. There was the energetic beautiful young woman of talent, in this case a singer, who rises to stardom, and then the repetition every few frames of we're going to have another child, and the husband beats her, or he sees other women, or he's dull in a willful, stubborn sort of way and she falls in love with another man; at any rate, she loses big—nervous breakdown, drugs, a domineering mother who takes over the children. And I told the nephew that I was afraid of that grown-up kind of life, that I didn't know why people submitted to it when it never seemed to work. And for me—so ordinary, with no talents to speak of and no direction, average looks— there was nothing at all. And the nephew ran his finger across his lip in a slow sort of way and said something, I can't remember exactly what; I'd had a lot to drink by that time, and we were surrounded now by noisy veterans spending their disability checks, floating around our table like rowdy ghosts. In the next breath he asked what I wanted from him, and I had no answer, no idea where anything was going. I would let him decide.

He motioned to the bartender and paid the tab. He put his hand on my arm as we left, and I was breathing so hard I couldn't talk though I remember laughing, and when we got in the car he pulled me over so I could lean my head against him but he didn't kiss me, I remember that. His breathing was deeper too, and regular, like sleep, and I could see his collar bone moving, and I tried to match my breathing to his.

I asked where we were going. He drove to the hospital. It blazed like a hospital. In there someplace David did some sort of office thing. He was doing it then. The lawn stretched around me; I was dizzy from the risk.

He led me through a metal service door into the basement. An old man in a striped pillow-ticking bathrobe sat in a chair by the exit sign. He was asleep, a straw hat in his lap. Every morning, the nephew said, he goes out with that chair, the hat, and a pole; all day he fishes on the rolling lawn. He slept there surrounded by pipes and wires and dust. Upstairs in the light old lungs sucked in oxygen, old veins sucked blood through long straws. Of course, I thought, looking at the man; what else can save you?

We walked past a table of veterans playing poker by a boiler. Through caverns of concrete and pipes and the smell of that dry red cleaner janitors with push brooms used to push around the hallways of grade schools. Now and then the warm, dim lights from pop machines in the corner of a room. The roaring of air and water from furnaces and pumps. A few dusty half-windows, the green of old Coke bottles.

He led me past bins of bleached white towels, through a storeroom filled with soap, into a laundry where black water throbbed against the glass fronts of the washers. There was

that clicking and scraping of snaps and buttons in free fall.
The concrete floor was slick. I slipped and almost fell. He put
his arm around my shoulder. I was shivering.

On the other side of the laundry was an empty storeroom. Someone had left a carpenter's level on a shelf. It was
coated with dust, the bubble off center in the chartreuse
liquid. I picked the level up, dusted it off. I tried to center the
bubble, but the slightest movement sent it floating. I played at
balancing the level on my hand like a baton. I threw it in the
air and watched it spin. I was that kind of night-time-bright-
lights giddy where everything seems brilliant, that kind of
giddy that's close to hysteria.

There was a butter-soft fold of skin beneath each of his
eyes. The room was so dark. Above our heads, the hospital
was an acre of solid rock. I asked him if many of his patients
died. He said that some of them did. I asked him if he knew,
when he took the patient from the doctor, if the patient was
dead or still sleeping.

Come on through here, he said, and I put the level down.
He opened another service door to the outside and we
climbed up some stairs, through cobwebs, until we were
looking at a square of sky. In front of us was a blue swimming pool surrounded by a wrought-iron fence.

It's August, he said. In another week they'll drain this,
close it up for the winter.

The water was lit by gold buttons from underneath, that
beautiful blue pool water, that blue blue ether. We sat on the
edge with our feet in the warm water. I reached over and
touched his hair, his face. I want you to know you're doing
this, he said, that this is real. The water glowed like neon.

He put his hand on my hair and pulled me to him. He
had this smile like a mischievous child. We slid down into the
pool and it was like floating down from a high place for

miles, we dove under the water, down to where it was gold and blue and tropical, and the rest of the world was nothing but a silvery skin on the surface.

I looked at the nephew then, and it occurred to me that I could live my life there, that I would never have to come up for air.

And that's when I ran. My legs shoved hard against the bottom of the pool, pushing me up through the water, the crystal blue water, into the gray of the Illinois night. And I ran back down the steps, through the basement, across the lawn, past decaying benches and warped picnic tables, underneath trees filled with ringing insects, and into the world of sad old men leaning on billiard cues, of office lights, of indecision, of chrome and neon, of women sorting through the debris, and all around me cars speeding by.

I don't know how I feel about the nephew now. I only know I will never be like Mina. I will never be the needle he threads, never the loom he drives his shuttle through. I'm more like the women behind the tables, distracted, starting projects and never finishing.

The nephew's still around. Others have seen him. I've seen his image in craft shows, in bake sales and church bazaars, in the faces of young girls and of businessmen, in my husband's easy walk. At times he's a tyrant. At times he gives life. I don't know. I only came that close to him one time. In that one place in Illinois. In the one and only August of my twenty-first year.

QUINELLA

He said his pay was heavy in his wallet. Let's
go, he said, over the river into Kentucky to the
races. Is it open? I asked. The horses stop running
early in the winter and don't come back until
spring.

They have this new thing, he said. It's all
televised.

Then why not stay home? I asked.

Why do you go to movies? he said. It's the
communal thing.

He drove like crazy through town, out of the
lights and into the country, taking the roads so fast
I thought we would spin. I opened the window
and let the air rush in.

Do you ever think about dying? I said to the
open window, and my words flew back into my
mouth.

He said that he did, that it gave him this start now and then, it was a physical thing, he said, like when you wake up fast from a nightmare or you start to go to sleep when you're driving and you pull back from somewhere fast.

Sometimes I'll see something common, he said, like a postage stamp with a picture of Eisenhower, and instead of thinking, Oh there's Eisenhower, I'll think instead, Oh there's someone who's dead, and I'll get this hard physical shudder like someone is shaking me.

Except for when I'm in a car with you, I said, I hardly ever think of it. So why am I here? I asked him.

Other times, he said, I feel like I'm skating over the surface of something. And then I'll think it doesn't matter. It really doesn't matter. We're all dead anyway. We're nothing but light. We just fade away.

He looked over at me. Look at the road, I said.

You're with me because you need me, he said. More than just about anything.

He drove faster through the country until he came to the black river, the bridge this black iron cage above it. It was a narrow road across the river, an old bridge, seldom travelled. People hardly ever left town this way, and no one ever came in.

Watch this, he said.

The dashboard lights lit his teeth. His hair was as wild as grade school pictures of Vikings. He turned the lights off and the road went black.

It was a cloudy night, no stars. We headed for the bridge. Below it, the dark Ohio.

It's dark, he said. Above. Below. Inside.

We reached the bridge and the ground disappeared.

I looked down but it was too dark to see the water. My God, I heard myself say. Open your fucking eyes.

I heard this sound come from my mouth like screaming. The bridge sped by. We were almost through the bridge
before it registered that he'd taken his hands off the wheel as
well, and when we hit the land driverless and blind it was
no more secure than the lack of it.

I reached over and grabbed the wheel from him. We
swerved away from an approaching car heavy on the horn,
its brights flashing.

He opened his eyes and turned on the lights. He laughed
and said the lights were blinding. You could have killed us,
I screamed at him, we could be dead at the bottom of the
river. He just smiled and said he knew what he was doing. I
thought, he said, it would be good for you. That was it, the
biggest shudder. It's over and behind us now, buried at sea.

It's either that, he said, or you sleep or shiver through
your life, and you might as well go back where you came
from and give someone else a chance to live it.

I hunched down, my knees slammed into the dashboard. He drove now with both hands. For the rest of the
trip he stayed in the right lane, he didn't tailgate, when he
passed another car he checked his blind spot. He talked in-
cessantly. I tried to tune it out.

When it was time to brake, my right foot slammed
down onto the floorboard. When it was time to shift gears, I
pushed in on the clutch. I told myself if we made it to Hen-
dersonville I would take a bus or hitchhike or blow every
cent I owned on a taxi home.

We came to a strip of fast food and stop lights, made a
few turns and we were at the racetrack, bright and expansive
as an airport. He stopped at the gate and paid the dollar for
parking.

It was a white stone parking lot, noisy as popcorn, and
we were late. We had to park in the back by the fence.

When the car stopped and he jumped out, I just sat there. I don't have any bones left, I said to him, no muscles, I can't move. He opened my door with a comment about chivalry, all slick irony, and he jumped up in the air and spun once completely around, then bowed and gave me his hand. M'lady, he said.

I slid my knees out, both knees together with my hands guiding, like an invalid. It felt familiar and it occurred to me it's how I'd been taught, at some lesson for girls, that a lady alights from a car.

I sat for another second with my legs dangling, my hand on the door. I didn't trust him, I realized, not to smash it shut. He reached down and put one hand on my shoulder, the other on my arm. He guided me up. His face swam up close.

You're a lunatic, I hissed at him. Certifiable. Insane. I'm never going a single place with you again.

His eyes reflected the pinkish-orange mercury lights from the parking lot. Looking at his eyes was like looking in a furnace.

I started walking, fast, for the squares of white light at the entrance to the track. I felt like I'd just recovered from a long illness, that kind of weak. My ankle kept rolling to the side on the uneven rocks. I felt his hand on my waist. I pulled away from him and went to the door on my own power.

I took my own money out of my own pocket and paid my three dollars. I walked right by the man handing out the programs. I didn't buy a racing form. I ignored a woman selling some expert's picks. I went to the shortest line and when I got to the front I picked the five and the eight Quinella. I didn't care about the odds. I took my ticket and went in the bathroom, where he couldn't follow me. I sat down by the coarse-haired woman who passed out the paper towels, the one who sold candy and breath mints. I watched a

bleached blonde arranging the surface of her hair, a teenager in tight jeans and black eyeliner putting wedges of raisin
color underneath her cheekbones and sucking in her cheeks.
I'd stay in here the whole time, where it felt safe. Just women.
The sound of all that whooshing water running through
pipes, the ka-thunk of the Tampax machine, all the slick
shiny lipstick, the smell of wet paper towels wiping off the
black wreaths of mascara underneath the eyes. In here where
it was light and familiar. There could be a nuclear holocaust
outside and it wouldn't matter; in here there was enough to
keep you alive for days.

I took my comb out of my purse and dragged it through
my hair so I wouldn't look suspicious. I hadn't washed the
comb in a while, and it smelled like iron filings.

The bleached blonde put a quarter in the old woman's
cup when she left. The teenager walked right on past her.

The race started, and the bathroom emptied except for
me and the attendant. Her eyes glazed over as she listened,
and she started this rhythmic rocking.

Toward the end of the race she snapped her fingers in
perfect time to keep things steady, to push the moment ahead
of her like an ice scraper, the horse leading her through time.

Come on seven, she said, come on seven, come on seven.

The click click of her fingers, she was as tied to the horse
as the jockey. Come on seven.

For all her snapping, the eight pulled ahead, her timing
off. She sped up the clicking in desperation, never abandoned
it even as the six gained ground and then the five. As though
the clicking, like the beat of the horse's heart and hooves,
could control its movement.

At the end of the race she gave this shrug, waited
through the photo for the miracle that would disqualify the
three leads and leave her gloriously on the finish line, then

tore her ticket in half and counted the change in her plastic cup.

Well, I said to her, that six stuck its head in the middle of my quinella, ruined my party, came between me and my new fur coat, my stainless steel Delorean, my college education, my Fortune 500 company, my summer home on Lake Michigan.

I ripped the ticket in half and she took it from me, threw it in the plastic lined bag by her feet. I gave her two dollars for her trouble.

It always does that, she said, the six. It's always the six, often the eight, sometimes the five when you're betting on the seven. I should learn, she said, shaking her head, that if I think it's the seven to bet on the six. If I think it's the eight to bet on the four.

I'm never right, she said.

She picked up a racing form from the floor beside her. Someone had thrown it away. There was a cigarette burn in the middle of the page, brown soggy coffee on the corners.

She stared at it then took out a pencil and did some figuring. She stepped outside for a second to look at the tote board. She handed me the two dollars back.

On this next race, she said, could you put this for me on the three to win? It's an overlay, she said. The experts pick it higher than the board. A good bet.

I took the money and went back out into the hazy smokey cavern. It was the least I could do for a fellow traveller. One minute till post time and the lines were moving fast, people shouting out their numbers, the guys who work the tickets stabbing their keyboards to take in as much money as they could before the boards shut down.

I saw the maniac three lines over, and I turned my head away from him so he wouldn't see me.

I put her two dollars on the three. I caught a glimpse of the maniac grinning at me. I started to walk away, then turned back to the ticket man. I put another two on the two and two on the four. I put two on the one and two on the five. Two on the six, two on the seven, two on the eight. The man had a cigar between his teeth; he looked at me like I was someone he'd seen before. You're one of those who wants a sure thing, he said.

I spent every penny I'd brought with me and took the tickets back to the attendant. Here, I said, a gift. Sometime in your life you deserve a win.

She took the tickets and looked through them. Her hand trembled. I couldn't cover the nine, I said, I ran out of money.

But it's outside, I said, he's a longshot, the nines have farther to run.

She looked at me hopefully, her hand still trembling. Maybe, she said. But with my luck it's the best night of that nine horse's life.

Post time and the bathroom cleared again. The race started and we sat there, relaxed.

The nine broke stride in the second turn and had to move to the back and start over. He would never catch up. It was a sure thing. It didn't matter who won. There was no rocking, no finger snapping. We sat there like royalty being served an eight-layer cake in our honor. It didn't matter in the least which layer we bit into first.

The race ended. I can't remember who won. I don't think we noticed. It wasn't the three. It was a favorite, only brought in three dollars and sixty cents, whatever its number. I handed all the tickets to the cashier and asked him to sort it out. I took the three dollars and sixty cents back to the woman. It's more than I would have got on the three, she said. I'm one dollar and sixty cents ahead for the first time in my life.

I was sixteen dollars behind.

I figured it out, how much I would have won if I'd bet all six to show, and it was nine dollars and forty cents.

Every sure thing is costly, I said to her, in this world.

She laughed and patted my arm like I was an infant who didn't know things.

She didn't ask me to place any more bets. She handed me a bar of chocolate candy. I unpeeled the whole thing from the foil and ate it. I was surprised at how hungry I was. It didn't begin to fill me up.

While I was at the sink washing the chocolate from my hands, I saw the attendant talking to the bleached blonde. She must be a regular, I thought, checking on all that hair. The attendant handed her two dollars. When the next race started she was back in a trance, rocking and clicking her hands.

I went back out into the crowd. There was so much smoke it was like I had cataracts.

The concrete floor was covered with tickets that hadn't come in. Pools of spit that looked like spilled Coke.

I watched a man throw away an empty box of popcorn and open a roll of lifesavers. He used the waxy string on his teeth like dental floss.

I ran through the crowd to the trackside door. The fresh cold air outside and only a few people just standing by the rail like I was, pulling it all in. There was no smell of horses, no hoofprints on the dirt.

I turned around to look at the building, two stories of glass. All the people inside bunching around the televisions for a race from New York, large screen TVs in front of the windows on the second floor. Everyone sitting in the rows of bleachers watching it all as comfortably as they would have real horses.

And I watched the crowd, the constant motion, the in-

dividual changing of places. Then the surge like one body
at the end of the race, the leaping and coming together like
clumps of cells.

I felt myself start to shudder. It was cold out here, too
cold. Somewhere in that crowd, the maniac was shouting.
The attendant in the women's room, clicking her fingers.
Any of us could have died on the way here, and it would
have been no less exuberant. The crowd healing over our
space. Filling it in.

THE INCREASING DISTANCE

Calm, and in a silence that was loud and thunderous, I gazed into his face.

Harry Houdini

The man who killed my brother owned the junk store where my brother cruised for things. The man assumed he was unknown to anyone. In this and other cases, he was wrong.

Let me tell you.

Once my brother repaired an old telegraph, part of it cherry wood, and he learned Morse Code so he could talk with his fingers. For a solid month, every night he tapped at it. There wasn't a single person listening. And still, all night long, dots and dashes, his fingers spoke. He said it felt like praying, all those words going out and no answer coming back to him.

Before his death, he was unlike any brother.

For as long as I remember, my brother collected things. His room was like an underwater cave, lit by a wall of bubbling aquariums and a green watery globe he bought at a yard sale; he said it was from a wrecked train's sleeping car. The globe was stuck to his wall like a scaly hard-shelled insect, its light buried down deep in the middle. That thick pop bottle glass, the light a smear of firefly goo.

Against one wall he placed steel shelving, like a warehouse, and filled it with old radio equipment and box cameras and waffle irons, with metallic mixers and tea kettles, a wall of shiny silver. Someone someplace had thrown each thing away. My brother knew and loved each curve of each metallic surface.

As we loved him.

My brother healed objects. Not like a repairman or mechanic; it was more than that.

The first thing was a fiddle from a dead great uncle.

When a neighbor saw it on our dining room table, she remembered a dulcimer with broken strings, and an autoharp with two broken pegs that she kept in the attic.

My brother loved the hollow sound of seeds in gourds. He could listen for hours to the click clack clicking of birds. Everything in this world was precious to him.

He found a rusted mouth harp in a junk heap on his way to school, and a rusted harmonica in another. Soon people were bringing over saxophones with chipping metal, the old clarinets resting in velvet-lined coffins that had been hiding out in the backs of closets. Anyone who brought him

an instrument offered it with relief and left feeling lighter.
This, they would say, this *guilt* has been lying around my
house for years, waking me up in the middle of the night
with its quiet, reproaching me every time I open the closet
to choose a morning shirt. There's nothing worse than an
abandoned trumpet, one man said. Oh yes there is. A vio-
lin with a broken bridge and strings that fly out like a jack in
the box, his wife said, that's a million million million times
worse.

Soon his room smelled like old chrome and rusted
screens. It was like an operating room, with sick violins and
trumpets reclining on tables, and he was the physician. He
restrung the cellos, put the guitars in vises to straighten the
necks. He used any money that came his way for parts or to
purchase other instruments: children's kazoos and penny
whistles, even pitch pipes.

He ran across a box of trombone mouthpieces at a
garage sale. For a week he would pick one up and make the
loudest elephant bleating sound he could make with it. The
cold metal would leave a white ring across his mouth that
would flush, immediately, with blood.

It was like a plague of instruments, and they kept coming
even after he was gone. At night now I'm the one who hears
them humming, who hears their strangled voices down
inside the valves and bells.

For one summer, my brother levitated tables. It was
nothing particularly magical. Like Dr. Dolittle and animals, he
just had some kind of feel for things. Once, in middle school,
he and his friends were playing with a Ouija board, lifting
each other with one finger, playing solitaire with tarot cards,
and for a joke, they turned off the lights and tried to make the
table rise.

It was terrifying when it did.

They experimented and found that not every combination of boys worked until, little by little, it turned out that my brother was the one who had to be in any group. And so, by agreement and without telling him, they took their hands off the table at once, and he sat there with his eyes closed, dark hair down below his shoulders then.

When he opened his eyes, he was the only one standing, his hands on the table, the table moving on the slightest cushion of air across the room.

And then for a while he dated girls and the tables, jealous, wouldn't move for him.

My brother was very handsome. His eyes were that kind where you can see the white part all around the iris, they were that large, and his flesh so pale against the dark hair it seemed like ice.

When my brother disappeared, my mother became, somehow, like those tables. She stayed in her bed too late in the day, in that ice blue nightgown in those ice blue sheets with the frost an inch thick on the inside of the windows from the condensation of her breath. She had called the police, the paper, and they didn't respond to her. Lady, they said, if we reported every gay runaway, the paper would be full of them. He's not a gay runaway, she said. He's not a runaway, she said. He's my son.

They took his name and information, and we sent them dental records and the fingerprints my mother had him make, one summer at a mall when he was twelve years old, and that was the last we heard from them.

Sometimes I want to take the remote control from the television and point it at the men who said that to her. Click it and then sharpen the focus, add more red, and press the

pause button to find that it's been on for months, a toggle
switch! and a second pressure would put them all back in
motion. Why can't you do that with people?

Sometimes when I lie in my room at night my thoughts
are so murderous I'm afraid they've taken form outside my
head, that they've seeped out in this scrim-like fog, all these
scenes playing out. What's wrong with me? I feel drunk
with all this, quite drunk with it. And afraid that something
filling me this completely is there for everyone to see, and
I jump when my mother comes into my room or tries to
watch some program I'm watching or reads over my shoulder, afraid that my thoughts have taken on substance, that
they're outside in the air with a sound and texture, and
anyone could touch them.

My brother knew things. He told me there's a galaxy
called the Great Attractor, and it's pulling us toward it. He
said the universe was formed in an explosion. He said that
we began in junk and joined some endless rush out from the
center. There's an increasing distance, he said, between every
single thing. You're younger than I am, he said. You'll live to
see I'm right.

Don't tell me things like that, our mother said to him, it
makes my mind go dim. I've sacrificed a certain amount of
joy in my life, she said, and in return expect a certain amount
of kindness. Blindness? my brother asked, mis-hearing her.
No kindness, she would say.

There were things he would never tell my mother.
Sometimes there has to be a deep chasm between the inner
world, my brother said, and the apparent one. It's not hy-
pocrisy. There's a certain amount of politeness involved in
appearance-keeping, he said, a wish not to offend. And a
measure of kindness, he said; our mother's right in that. You

make an adjustment here and another there, and soon you're living a double life.

It's the thing my brother had in common with the man who killed him.

What was all my brother's knowledge for? He taught me to look for the pale insects, like bits of burning paper, that hover above the evergreens in winter. You'll see them for a second, he'd say, and then in the right or wrong light, with a shift of the head one direction or the other, they disappear as though they were never there.

The man who killed my brother owned two houses. He abandoned one in favor of another, one summer in a stream of newfound money. He took his wife and children with him.

For months, after my brother disappeared and the bones were discovered and the man who killed my brother killed himself, I drove by that abandoned house, trying to understand it. The gutter falling off and at an angle, old husks of at least four cars in the driveway and the garage, one of the cars low slung and covered with the moldy shroud of a canvas tarp, like some old vegetable left too long in the refrigerator.

I should say that his was not a neighborhood where houses were abandoned, or cars for that matter, or bodies. At night, even when the occupant of a house was on vacation, lights clicked on in one window or another, and every soul had a metallic set of wheels to whisk it to work or school or shopping, and when someone died, the flesh was moved to a proper graveyard with a brick fence, and the children spent their days in school.

I watch the people in their houses, and they seem like sleepwalkers to me.

The yards of these houses are filled with giant trees, and they spread out around each house like a small park. In August, the tree locusts scream, their sound as shrill as bombs. How could you live with that sound and not wake up? Why didn't anyone know him well enough? Why don't they talk about it now? We sacrifice a certain amount of joy, my mother said. Blindness, my brother said back to her.

The children knew something was wrong. What kind of car is under that tarp? I asked a neighbor boy, knowing he would know. The neighborhood kids stuck their tongue in the abandoned house over and over, like a bad tooth. They'd been in the A-frame playhouses out back, in the garage, underneath the tarp, sitting in the seat of the car with portable CD players, listening to songs with titles like "Irresponsible Hate Anthem." "Let's just kill everyone," I heard one singing, "and let God sort them out."

The boy had a sweet voice, sweet face, sweet strawberry blond hair. Innocent hair.

It's no kind of car, he said. Used to be a Porsche, but the engine's gone; now it's just the shell of a Porsche. It's nothing.

It was everything I could do to keep from asking what was in the playhouse, the garage, the cathedral-ceilinged living room.

Old tires, he volunteered. Rusted potbellied stoves and several cars in the garage. Broken things. Mannequins standing around the kitchen with their arms raised, frozen, he said, like grown-ups at a party.

There were sixteen acres on the horse farm where they found the fragments of my brother's body. Bone slivers, the flesh burned away by fire. For months dogs had been bringing bones into the neighbors' houses. From someone's trash, each neighbor said. It couldn't be imagined. I didn't know, the wife told a reporter. We worked together twenty-four hours a day when we owned the business, and I never suspected a thing. Am I naive? she asked. I didn't know, when we got

married, what courses he took in college, what he was ma-
joring in. The first year of our marriage he ended up in a
mental hospital for six months, and I never asked him why. I
simply loved him. People are too quick, she said, to judge the
quick and then the dead.

All his children are in middle or early high school. It was
a month after the father shot himself, several months after
they discovered the bones in their back yard, six months
before they pieced the first four bodies together from some of
the bones. My brother was one of them. There were pictures
in the morning edition of eight other missing men.

The running of that store, the wife said later, took up
twelve hours of every day, being a mother the rest of her
hours. She had very little time for sleep. Detail by detail ate up
all those hours, she said.

I had no idea, she said later, what my husband was
doing. I had no idea, she said, that men did those things with
men. Which sounded false, I thought as I read it, her saying
that. Or simple-minded. And if simple-minded, then how did
she spend twenty-four hours a day with him, as she said, and
run the finances? If not simple-minded, then deliberately
deceptive. And if not deliberately deceptive, then what is a
marriage that you could live with someone for twenty-five
years, have three children, and know so impossibly little
about the most important things that went on inside the
bony box of your husband's skull.

My son had his secrets, my mother always said. But I
would recognize him anywhere.

The mother and the children moved back into the
abandoned house in October, a yellow topaz clear October,
never a cloud the whole month, the kind of weather that
mocks you if you're not happy. They raked their leaves and

put them into pumpkin trash bags, just like everyone, turning the trash into a decoration. They moved their day-to-day maintenance stuff—the toothpaste, the hairbrushes and clothes and food—in among the old tires in the living room and the mannequins. They left a blond fifties housewife mannequin staring out the front hall window for several weeks, apron on, arms posed like Donna Reed. It called attention to itself. Why didn't she remove it? If you're not looking for strange, she said in the paper, you don't see strange.

Don't hate her, my mother says, and in this my brother would have agreed with her. Forgiveness came easily for him, and for my mother. You live in a world that strange for so long, and it begins to seem like normal life, my mother says. You wake up one morning and look around and notice that none of your neighbors keep books in their oven or plastic soulless bodies looking out the front of the house. But at some point, early, I say, you noticed it. And then decided not to. The imagination wants, I say to her, this terrible accuracy.

I read about a rock from Mars with fossilized pieces of organic matter. Maybe in all that dust there used to be a garden. Bacteria in space and then that life form they found deep in the ocean that doesn't require any oxygen to live and that giant fungus that broods and dreams under the state of Michigan. What does it mean? There are days I'd love to roll my brain up into a little condensed ball and slide it down through my throat and along the right arm to the tips of my fingers, where I'd meld into this keyboard and the pain would disappear.

It's so difficult to carry, this flesh, this body. I read someplace that if you drop a photo negative in bleach, the smoky image fades and you're left with clear acetate, something you can see through. And when you want a photo negative that won't leech away no matter how much bleach you throw it in, you etch platinum into fused quartz: quartz fused, that is, to other quartz.

I like to imagine a planet of platinum and quartz existing completely outside the loop of biology, completely eternally there, though my mind goes numb when I try to imagine where I'd put it, beyond the edge of this expanding exploding thing they call the universe. Which would be, as I imagine it, something absolutely still and warm and filled with light and music. Something, I realize as I'm saying it, like a house. Surely God has provided such a place, a quiet unchanging place in all this oozing darkness. A house that would hold my platinum and quartz planet on a shelf in absolute and perpetual stillness. That's all I want, that stillness. And to know that something's holding me even more securely than a mother's arms.

I would replace the parts of my body bit by bit with these non-biodegradable limbs, little by little until I was left the essential part, the one thing I couldn't be me and live without, whatever that thing is. I imagine you could replace part of the brain with computer chips, but there might be some little glistening cell all slick like an oyster, some slick blue smear you couldn't live without. Then I'd know I'd isolated the soul.

I'd place that slick cell on my silver planet inside my quiet house alongside the single cells of the people I love. And we would all stay there smiling at each other. My brother, our mother. Our father. And not a one of us would ever die.

In the winter, the giant hostas melt down immediately on the day of the first frost. The green leaches out or it's like they're covered with a grayish film, and they lie there limp on

the ground, like boiled greens, but there are these beautiful
markings on the leaves, a complicated system of roads. On
the day the first frost boils down the hostas, I walk outside to
look at them and I think about the way dead people look,
that same gray, that same unmoving.

When the body dies, the skin turns gray, the pupils large
as plates, blotting out the color of the iris. Black and shades of
gray and white. The power of black-and-white photographs,
my brother told me once, is in the sense of movement flickering underneath death's landscape. As a person dies, the senses
turn off one by one like television screens until you're left
with breathing, heart-beat, then that too clicks off.

On Halloween, the daughter looked just like the pictures
in the paper of her father, but she had a kind sweet smile, and
she passed out chocolate candy.

They called him the Bone Man, and the neighborhood
children rallied around his children. Everyone's parents, one
boy explained to me, are strange. Everyone's parents lie. For
instance, he said that half his friends were living with step-
parents who hit their lives with the force of a truck going
through a red light and broadsiding their minivans. Did the
parents give the kids any advance warning? Nah, the boy
said. They just lied until the truck smashed through the
windshield.

Disguised as a child, I dressed as a genie, rainbow-colored
sequins on my costume. The girl I walked with painted her
face white with fake blood gashes across the cheeks. The
blood was peeling off like crayon wax, leaving just her white-
washed face, disconcertingly lovely as a geisha.

How beautiful, everyone said as they came to the doors
and saw the two beggar girls. The little girl would growl

and moan at them; she knew she was supposed to be terri-fying.

A geisha's face, like a monster's, doesn't register the ebb and flow of blood to the pores, the human being under-neath the skin.

We talked to a girl who lived next door. Her brothers had spent the night there, often, with the Bone Man's son. When we left the Bone Man's house, the girl stopped at the sidewalk and looked back, her sequins sparkling in the streetlight. When I talk about this, she said, I'm afraid I'll hurt her. She was referring to the Bone Man's daughter.

There were mannequins, mostly male, around the family's indoor pool in the country. This isn't strange? No, the wife said, not strange. It was security against the real strangeness: the bad-man with an axe who comes inside in the dark of night to rape your wife and steal your money and your children.

Most of the murders were strangulations, by garden hose. By her husband's hands. (In the paper they showed those hands, kind father's hands, feeding his infant children Cream-of-Wheat.)

Some of the strangulations took place in that pool, those giant dolls looking on. Knock the arm off a doll, decapitate it, and there's never a response.

When our father died, my brother found his body. Our father was living alone then, divorced from our mother. My brother broke into the house, all the lights blazing, the radio playing classical music. He was lying in bed, his glasses on the kitchen table by his cold morning coffee.

In the weeks that followed, there was no way to talk about our father's death except to say that he'd passed on. To

what? I believe as my brother said, that the universe began
with the big bang and ends in entropy. In between, I think
about how he loved us and how sad it makes me now when
it rains or is cold and he's there in the ground with no one to
put a blanket over him. When I think about my neighborhood I think about how he once lived here and now isn't
living.

The day my brother found our father, he said he was
most aware of whatever it was that animated him and how
that flame was gone, that fire in the face. For two or three
days, he said, he saw it in every human face, and the mystery
of it was unfathomably strange to him. For three days only.
On the third day of grieving you rise up temporarily from
the dead and whatever wisdom you gained from it is gone.

*Is this the proper moment for the grand finale? Crack! Right here,
right now is when the light should flicker out. Did you see it? It's hard to
see. It was there and now it's gone and the body is a puppet with no pup-
peteer, no strings, the mass of cells gone suddenly heavy in his arms. The
pool, bouyant and blue as an aquamarine. For a while the water holds
the body like the sky. When he takes the boy out of the water, there's
what's left to dispose of. Out in the woods, underneath the leaves; in less
than a year the soil will do its work, it's what it's about, it's what it's
there for. Not a single soul will miss him.*

*And again: There's the boy's soul pushed up against the face, filling
each feature in the face. And then, with a snap, it's gone. But I didn't get
it, he thinks. A precise man, meticulous man. One more time, he thinks,
and he'll catch the sight of it in the blind spot. Where did it go? he won-
ders. At which precise moment did it flicker out? And what was it, what
was the it? Is this boy a mass of singular cells or is he greater than the
sum of these parts? And what am I? A monster. And will this mon-
strousness go on and on.*

* * *

At what moment did the joy leave the new purchase—brocade pillow, sweater, clear glass vase—the container of that joy left on the front porch in a trash bag, to be driven to the store and sold again, the smell of the human who owned it ground into the fibers of cloth, ghosts of fingerprints on the glass and metal.

There was no blood, the wife said in the paper, no mud on the tiles, no smell of smoke or filled ashtrays, no sign of any of it.

The Bone Man's wife stands outside in the thick mud of December. She wears brown boots and a red coat. She wraps wires strung with thousands of tiny lights around the leafless bushes. Six months after her husband's suicide, and she will have the house ready for Christmas. He cannot take that from her. She refuses to let him take that from her. She will wrap toys for her children Christmas morning.

The day after Christmas, trash bags line the curved streets like luminarias. Filled with crushed boxes, Christmas in and out: last year's dolls, hair tangled and pulled at the roots, stuffed animals missing eyes, the nap worn, last year's now-unfashionable clothes, all left along the street to be carted away, this guilt, in the rain, this guilt; what do we do with it?

The store was in a strip mall that used to be a virgin forest. The strip mall is by a string of other malls that stretches from the east to the west side of the city. The last forty acres of woods has been rezoned to allow for another strip mall. The man who heads the zoning commission is also on the board of the development group that's building the new mall.

Part of that mall will be a grocery store. The vast array of prepared foods in the new deli. The delicious crust on the

warm bread. The fresh coffee in complimentary cups. The
sweet hum of the dairy cases. The butcher's skill.

There's a grocery store one block north, owned by the
same company. It will be closing down as soon as the new
one is built. I've lived in this city my entire life, and I know
what will happen. Immediately, the old building will begin
its slow decay. The windows will crack, the pipes will freeze.
The rectangles of black dirt and goo where the freezer cases
stood. The lights will break and bleed across the parking lot.

Just west of the new strip mall is an entire neighborhood
recently made from a golf course which was recently made
from farmland which was recently made from a forest so
dense it echoed the darkness of the sky when the carrier pigeons made their northward migration.

Like the pigeons there are, we sometimes think, too
many of us. The developer for all these projects lives in the
Bone Man's neighborhood. He is in all respects but this one,
a good man. There are speakers outside his house, for the
stereo, disguised as moon rocks.

We will all take our things home and briefly cherish
them. Everything, it seems, is made to be ephemeral. We are
all made in God's image, my brother often told me. He would
forgive, I think, everything but the silence. In that, he would
say, we're all of us guilty.

Which brings me back to love.

I remember one Christmas when my brother and my
father were still with us. An ice storm that sounded like a
hard summer rain, or like pieces of plastic trees that model
airplane parts come on, all falling to the floor at once. And
then a snow, which was quiet and odd. The corners of the
windows glazed with melting triangles of ice, now and then a
chunk of snow falling from the top branch of a pine tree illu-

minated by floodlights, then an explosion of powdered ice that hits the window glass before turning to liquid.

We were children.

My brother and I went outside about midnight, when the snow stopped, to see the snow, clean and pure, a purply magenta tinge from vapor lights and from a purple neon tube in the window of an all-night bakery across the alley.

On a table inside the window there were rings of dough rising in the heat, so like the texture and weight of human flesh. They lay there in the warmth, on the tin pans, glazed with sugar and icing, rising. Rising! Five days before Christmas.

We walked around to the back yard, thin flecks of ice swirling in the air, the snow blowing from the drifts, the breath of the house behind him in the dark, five days before Christmas. We were children.

And there in the alley between the houses we saw our father, a long gray coat with the collar pulled up to his chin against the cold, hands in his pockets. He was stalking something, slow slow cat movement and then a strange leap backward, all elbows and knees and then the slow sideways movement, circular.

At one point we saw him put his hand to his forehead and spin, and then the slow movement again toward whatever it was hidden behind the row of white pines and hawthorns and mulberry trees, with a few shriveled and frozen blackish berries.

Hey, my brother whispered, and our father put his fingers to his lips, shh. Hush now. Shh.

And he motioned us forward.

When we got behind the row of trees we saw it, there in the alley between our house and the bakery, and our hearts started beating, hard, the way I remember feeling one other time at Christmas in an amusement park, when I'd gone into a gingerbread house with the sun setting and come out the exact moment all the thousands of twinkling lights came on, and I felt as though I'd walked into heaven as easily as you'd walk into your own kitchen, just one step and there you were, no more steps, and the rest of time was simply gliding through colored lights and cinnamon and pine.

It was some kind of animal. White and small and still as death. Its head held up in the air though, so not dead. But that still. And the wind blew ice crystals into my brother's eyes, and they melted on our father's coat with all the colors of the rainbow, like diamonds.

Yes, my brother said then, yes, and he didn't go up to it, just circled around it, both he and our father in the middle of that kind of awe you feel sometimes, though rarely, and I wish I could even begin to explain to you how magical it seemed to us, how like some otherworldly thing that still white animal was for five minutes, maybe more. I can't say what we thought it was, whether from outer space or a messenger from God, just that it opened up immediately some part of us that spent all its time looking for magic. It wasn't even a feeling that this ghost animal was purely good. There was something terrifying about it, we knew, even horrifying, and still we opened up to it; we were prepared to worship its introverted stillness, circling with our father around the circle of its light.

My brother went near to it then, and nearer. It was his job in our family to be the brave one. Until he got within six inches of its skin and saw that it was in fact nothing but the plastic lamb from some old woman's nativity. My father started laughing. Some kid had picked it up and dropped it in the alley as a prank, or even not a prank, just something thoughtless.

Even so my brother shuddered, I noticed, as he picked it up, and the lamb that had seemed like plastic junk, something we paid no attention to, still kept a bit of that weird stillness as he walked it across the alley, through the swirling ice crystals and back to the old woman's yard. Dried vines covering the house, trumpet vine coated with ice so the trumpets looked like sugar-coated bells, wedding cake bells, and they clicked and clicked in the wind and shook their heads at him.

He put the lamb on the ground beside Joseph. Balthazar was lying on the ground, and my brother righted him. It was the middle of the night and the old woman's nativity was burning with floodlights. Jesus' skin was glowing from the inside with its own 25-watt bulb, the skin like soap, an imperfection in his left cheek where someone had chipped a bit of the plastic. And when I imagine my brother touching that cheek I imagine the dull echoless sound of his hand against the plastic, and I think of him lying there after he was murdered, with that same deep stillness.

Our father came then to where my brother was kneeling in the snow, and he took off his coat and put it around my brother's shoulders, and we went inside, stopping once by the hawthorn to clip branches and red berries glazed with dripping ice.

You're so brave, I whispered to my brother when he started crying, so beautiful, so beautiful, I said. He sat on the floor by a corner where the wall jutted out into the room, making one wall of light and one of shadow, and my brother there in front of it still shaking with the cold and the fear and something deeper that he'd fallen into, some darkness without any end, the glazed branches in his arms, the coat still around his shoulders and bunched up around his crossed knees, and even though my brother sat there cradling that wet wood, not even the sting of cold melting water brought

him back to the room. By then I think he'd realized that
whatever he'd seen, not the lamb itself, but the something in
him that was clearly always always waiting for something
that would never come was so frightening, that none of this,
none of it, nothing you did in this life, would ever matter.

You know how the magician David Copperfield makes
snow appear in his hands, how he shakes and shakes his
hands, those kohl-lined eyes staring at you, and soon he's
covered in a blizzard of it and the entire audience is covered
in ice crystals? I've seen it on television. It's all theatre, snow
machines hidden underneath the floorboards, in the theatre
walls, in the ceiling—the way they drop confetti and balloons, I don't know exactly how it's done. The only thing
you need in order to see it is to want to believe. We only ask
him to not make it too obvious. Lift me, we say, please, make
me fly, give me wonder and magic, give me love. Make it
seem real.

My brother was a fragile, thoughtful man. And for one
night, he brought that same mistaken faith to the Bone Man's
madness, his own fragility. He brought with him that heady
neon wish to leap, and the feeling that there was nothing in
the place he was standing, nothing he'd be leaving behind.

How easy it is to move slow step by slow step with
someone you perhaps irrationally love and trust into a world
you never knew existed. All those aches that opened up in
him that night, and later, when our father died. Like water
finding fissures in stone, the Bone Man filled them.

NIGHT TRAIN

At the trial they said that Madge had been abducted. But there were little details that didn't fit: the doorman at the Claypool Hotel who saw her waiting in the car without an escort. She waved at him in the light from the gas lamps. He remembered her hair, so black it was almost blue, and the wet shine on the pavement, veined by the metal tracks from the trolley. He said the smell from coal dust was thick that night, he said he'd been washing down the beveled glass in the door to the hotel for hours.

Steve had a will larger than this city, the kind of will it's almost impossible to escape from. I've known men like him. All it takes is single mindedness and narcissism and—what. Once I knew a cook who would put a speck of ground glass in the soup or cigarette ash in a sauce, just to know that he could. Not enough to hurt anyone, just so he would know it was there and he could watch an old man sip down bowls of chowder knowing there was that brittle bit of something that, if it were bigger, would begin to wear a hole inside large enough for his life to seep through.

This cook would look at the wet ground in the spring and watch the entire landscape loosen, unbuckle belts and fasteners and start to ooze around his feet, and he wanted to be the one who caused that loosening. Because he knew he could. He was a cook and when he looked at the world he saw it pressed into a fine string and woven through the bodies of people who knew in this world they would always be hungry. Once you know that, anything is possible.

That's how I see Stephenson and how I see Madge with him and that's how I think it happened. And I feel enormously guilty when I say that, going against the story of her abduction and rape by a man fully consciously evil. Who in this world ever sees himself as evil finally? No one. I think it was, instead, a loosening in the face of an enormous will, that she felt herself lifted into a whirlwind and then his voice, Steve's voice, saying, *listen girl, believe me when I tell you to close your eyes and fly and believe me when I say my arms are larger than the state, larger than God's, so large I can hold you up here where nothing will touch us, and I absolutely will not let you fall.*

He didn't say he loved her, just that and the fact that it was a quick shot to Chicago, the straight humming rails with car after car all coupled in a chain like the cells of her body like all the human beings and animals and atoms in the world coupling, separating, and reforming always with a kind of violence. And there she was, he said, maybe about to be left out of it or about to let go as she should, to take the freedom he was offering her. I'm sure his argument had some-

thing to do with courage. I'm sure she heard heroic music
playing. Otherwise where would she be? Straight rows of
church pews, of moment following moment, of stitches in the
hem of her good winter coat. The cemetery was filled with
row after straight fixed row of sinking stones.

They do sink, you know, after awhile, like rocks to the
bottom of a creek bed.

So Steve's driver took them to Union Station, and they
walked into that huge vault of arches and stained glass
and Madge felt something rise up in her as clear and high as
that ceiling, a giddiness or expansion of her self, like a cathe-
dral. You know I'm mad about you, he'd said, or something
like that, and they were heading for the train to Chicago and
some bit of work I'm sure he'd said they had to do there, so
the whole thing was this heady mixture of passion and duty.
She could picture all the rest of us, her sisters, sleeping in our
dull beds in the dull Midwestern night, the moon a fake
mother of pearl with the plastic peeling off the surface, sleepwalking through our lives. When they, Madge and Steve,
were in fact the ones sleepwalking. You know I'm mad about
your body, he said, and in this much he was conscious: he
knew he was seducing her.

I have to say this. The prosecuting attorneys painted her
as wholly innocent. I believe she was. But not in the way
they meant it. I do think that she started on this trip at least
partially willingly, that there were times, even in Chicago, that
she remained willingly. That doesn't make Steve less culpable.
It just makes it more human, something you could see yourself being somehow sucked into. It's why it doesn't work to
tell kids not to do something because they'll die. Then they're
not prepared for the seduction, for how good it feels, how
much they might want it, and when they find that out they
think that everything they've been told has been a lie. So I

think that a woman hearing the story of Madge dragged and bound in the middle of the night on a train to Chicago won't be prepared for anything. The dragged and bound kind of abduction—you can't see it coming, there's nothing you can do but work for some escape. But the kind that comes with power and charm, you think of it as a story outside and beyond you, not there in this particular smiling man. You know? Everyone loves him, even the governor. You feel so lucky that he turned to you. You! Madge Oberholtzer. A stenographer, working girl, with a life suddenly here in the dull center of the country like any New York flapper, the kind of life you read about in the magazines.

She had a beaded purse on her lap, with a handkerchief, some lipstick and powder, a pocket mirror. Why does that break my heart?

At one point on the train, maybe early on, maybe she felt the lens shift slightly from romance to something darker. And she laughed and said no to something he suggested, still living in that version of herself as the good Victorian girl with jazz-age courage, a difficult fiction to live behind as many girls like Madge discovered at that time, like a paper doll cut from paper made in two different centuries, the difficulty being that you have to find a man who isn't looking for the seam where the papers are joined, too flimsily, with makeshift glue. Madge and I were in the same sorority in college. I know what it was like then. The 1920s. We were born with the century. We really thought we'd invented sex. It's hard to believe now how innocent we were.

Why do I keep talking about innocence? Because this is a trial, and I have to come down on one side or another and I know that what I'm talking about is too human for that sort of certainty. Everyone has his own story, a story that's woven as tightly, that fits as warmly, as those footed pajamas that children wear.

Years ago I went rafting on the Little Pigeon River in Tennessee. It was a brilliant July day, not a cloud, everything shimmering like money. I was with a whole group of people, bobbing around on the Little Pigeon, a lot of chatting between rafts, a lot of falling and splashing in the water.

For a while I talked and then for a while listened and then finally, after an hour or so I just lay back on the raft and relaxed absolutely, letting the river and my fellow travellers take the raft and my thoughts without any direction from me—no paddling, no pushing against the shore, nothing—and after a half an hour there was this one moment when suddenly everything dissolved—the sky became the river, the river bled into the trees, I felt my body start to disintegrate into glittering pieces, or rather, I didn't feel my body as mine at all, what the Eskimos call kayak sickness, and I felt like I was falling into the sky. And suddenly there was this physical start, like the yank of a bridle, the bit in the corner of my mouth. That's up, that's down, this is upstream, that's downstream. These are the hard edges that separate one thing from another.

This has something to do with all of this, bear with me. I'm an old woman and allowed to wander.

My lover was with me on that trip, and that night when we came in from the carnival nightlife of Gatlinburg, the Little Pigeon outside the window of our room, I thought about the river and how there's a letting go that's terrifying. That if you could throw off the bridle, if you could trust that dissolution, if you trusted that your body was an especially strong and natural swimmer, then there would be this joy that might feel like drowning, like pain for a while but would eventually build this pressure and thrust you up through the endless water, or rather, through the brilliance of all the shimmering light, and you would rise up like the spouting foam of a great whale.

Or you could take something, a cup, and hold it in the fountain of that light, and drink it down, drain it into every cell.

I was madly in love, madly madly in love, and on that trip with my lover to the mountains and the thundering river, I started noticing when the bit of fear pulled me back, said that's good but enough, and I consciously, in the middle of each wave let go even more, a greater and greater letting go, and I swear to you one night I just stayed there floating on top of this sea for an entire evening, and it was something like coming, but deeper.

You don't want to hear this about an old woman, do you, but there you have it.

And you may think I'm getting back to Madge and Steve and that I'm going to say that's what Steve wanted. But what I'm going to say is that it's what Madge wanted, what she sensed and couldn't articulate, and that, in her innocence, she thought had nothing at all to do with love, that love was in fact the binding cord, the bridle.

And what Steve wanted? Not this letting go at all, that's exactly what he was most terrified of, no matter what he said. If he felt someone like Madge taking him close he'd feel like he was floating on a raging river and right ahead, with no turning back, the endless, pounding, falls. And that's when he sank his teeth into her, to pull himself back onto the shore. The autopsy showed them, on her breast. Puncture wounds caused by human teeth.

Did you know that at one time there were falls on the Ohio River? We domesticated them with locks.

I can't let go of the fact that she didn't tell her parents she was going to Chicago, that she didn't take anything with her for the trip. She left the house in her black wool coat, even

though the day had been sunny and spring-like, and she
didn't take a hat. She'd been out dancing with a friend, had
come into the house at 10 P.M. Her parents had both been ill
for a week with the flu; despite the early spring weather, and
the crocuses along the foundation of the house, they'd been
closed in, the windows still sealed tight, and the house had
that sickroom smell, and all week she'd noticed the dust in
the cracks of the wood floors and the sticky film on the furniture. They were old, her parents, and she lived there with
them, and when she shut the door on the night and felt the
contrast between the gay dance she'd left and the closed-in
house, and the flesh of her parents, and when her mother
said that Steve's secretary had called for her, had said for her
to call no matter what time she came in, Madge got on the
phone and said she'd be right there. There was moonlight
coming through the lace curtains in the entry hall, and the
dim chandelier glowed like cool stars. He needs me right
away, she told her mother, some papers I need to prepare.
He's leaving later on the train for Chicago.

She didn't say anything about going with him. How
could she?

Though maybe she was angry with them for some
reason, maybe she told herself she would call them the next
morning, and in fact she sent a telegram from a hotel in
Hammond. Or maybe it was kidnapping, and everything else
I've said applies to some other woman, not this particular
one.

However it was, she was in the car outside the Claypool with no one watching, thinking to herself maybe that
she shouldn't be doing this, that she would tell Steve that
when he came back to the car, she would tell him and he
would keep her on; they would still work on that project together, she'd still have the excitement of carrying messages for

him, of being associated with the most powerful man in
Indiana.

There was the yellow light from the inside of the hotel,
all refracted into pieces like flower petals or gold glitter, and
the light in the streetlamps and the headlights of cars, the
light caught in the bracelet on her wrist, a ring on her right
hand, some silver threads in her dress fabric. I wonder if she
thought about crosses burning out in the country, the gangs
of young men that Steve set in motion, I wonder what or
if she thought about those crosses, or if she even knew. She
worked in the department of education, it's said she was
compassionate, liberal, I wonder if she didn't know about
the things the Klan was doing, or what it was Steve told her
to stop her from worrying. Or if that was something she
thought she might change in him, if it was part of their
banter when they talked, something that attracted him to
her—the fact that she had her own mind.

The train station was busy, loud and dirty, even that late
at night, and the train to Chicago was almost full. He got two
private rooms, and for a while she thought that maybe it was
going to be all right, but when they walked through the railroad car in the warm domestic light of the stopped train, and
Shorty went into one room and Steve followed her to hers,
and he came inside with her, and locked the door behind
him, she knew that it wasn't going to be all right, but she realized she didn't care.

And then the roaring of the train on its bright rails, metal
against metal like sharpened knives, and Steve came toward her in the dim light of the car. They were moving, and
outside the window, all of Indiana was dark and somehow
oceanic, unfixed, a wilderness of fields waiting for spring
seeding. If she were outside, she knew, she could smell the

mud from spring thawing, in the morning there would be

the early sound of birds, it was March. She'd been waiting
months for the feel of spring, for the damp ooze of spring,
but here in the railroad car there was only speed and metal,
and the hard oilcloth seats and the thin mattress on what
served as a bed, like the beds, she thought, that men slept on
in prison.

I'm thirsty, she said, still feeling like a seduced one, which
implies a moment of giving in, thinking she had a choice still,
still not believing that she could be in any real danger. It was
a *game* of danger they were playing, and at any moment she
could say enough, let's stop this now, it was an adventure,
but I want to go home, I want the feel of my own soft bed,
the smell of clean sheets, my mother's voice and in the morning the bell of the phone and my girlfriends calling, and the
story I could tell them of how much you wanted me.

He turned out the light in the car, and there was only the
reflected light from the moon on his face, an ashen grayish
light, and from then on there would be only the occasional
light from a farmhouse or small town. His face was round
as the moon in fact, floating above her, his lips were too
full. He took a flask from his pocket and made her drink; he
wouldn't ask the porter for any water. In the dim light he
looked boyish with his pale blonde hair, boyish and swollen,
like someone's child. And she, Madge Oberholtzer, wasn't
there at all for him, she could tell that right away, his boyish
face, lost, his eyelids closing over the pale blue eyes, the half
smile on his face as he touched her. She was something just
ordered up on the table, a woman with wide hips and pink
aureoles large as platters. That's all he saw, or, rather, all he
felt. She believed she had an awkward face. It didn't matter.
Maybe she should accept this as the adventure it was. But
wasn't he at least supposed to say he loved her?

He had a baby face, dark shadows around his eyes, oval shadows like the slits in the white hoods of the Klansmen. She hoped that he would grow to love her.

The last thing she remembered being excited by was his face, by the picture she had of herself as brave, by the romance of the long dark train thundering like a river through the country. She was a little bit scared, but that was part of it. If pushed to the wall, she'd have to say she still trusted him.

I saw her two days later, an hour or two after Steve's bodyguard brought her into her parent's house. There were scratches all over her body. She was barely breathing. She told the story, whispered it. For three days the lawyer had her tell the story slow. There was a stenographer who typed it up at night and read it back the next day. Madge's dying statement. She had to say she knew that she was dying before she signed it. I was a witness to her signature.

At one point, in Chicago, she'd found his gun lying on a table. She stood in front of a full-length mirror and lifted the gun to her head. She thought about her mother then, the disgrace this kind of suicide would bring and somehow in her confusion, the lawyers said, decided on another way.

That's when she talked Steve into letting her go out with his assistant to buy the hat, and she went into the hat shop unescorted. This is another part of the story that never fit. And she tried hats on, several of them, perhaps looking for one that would cover the marks on her face, hoping to go back on the train maybe like any woman out for the day, not like the woman she felt was at that point, with the sky as blue and absolutely flat as enamel, red buds coating all the trees and somewhere a metallic bell-like sound that seemed to rise up out of the day itself, like that sound you get when you run a wet finger around the top of a crystal goblet, that kind of sound. She looked at herself in the mirror at the hat

store and she saw a Madge whose life would never be the same again. She felt nauseous and brittle, and there wasn't even the tiniest bit of magic in the hat. The mirror's glass was a yellow greenish gold. She looked like an old woman to herself, and she couldn't imagine living. This part is all conjecture. The lawyer only had the time and Madge the strength to gather facts.

She went into the pharmacy then, unescorted, by telling the bodyguard that she needed some female things, that she was bleeding. He'd been kind to her in the hotel room. He'd soaked white towels in warm water and applied them to the scratches and the bites, washing the towels out in the sink when they got too cool, the blood a pale pink. He was a kind man. He was clumsy with his nursing, embarassed and slightly deferent, the way she imagined a husband might be, so different from Steve. All that was closed off to her now. Steve gets like this, he said, I'm so sorry, but it's just the way he is, you know. We all have our failings, and this is his. He might have called the police or a doctor, but he was also a weak man, she could tell, and he owed everything to Steve, and he was slightly afraid of him. And he probably told himself that Madge wasn't a whole woman anyhow, not one of the women the Klan was defending, she was one of the other kind, slightly less than a woman since this had happened to her, a good woman who'd allowed herself to become a whore.

But he let her go into the pharmacy alone. And there was clearly no thought of escape. She could have leaned over to whisper a word to the pharmacist, but she didn't.

If she'd lived, we agreed, no one else would ever hear a word of this story. It would have just meant shame for her. She knew shame.

Mercury chloride is the drug she bought in the pharmacy. Maybe she had been a virgin before that night; maybe she was terrified of pregnancy only, her mind so clouded at that point with the beating that the only real shame she could imagine was the one she was familiar with. The physical evidence, like some disease. Mercury chloride was used in those days to induce abortions.

Maybe Steve's story was partially right. Maybe the initial tragedy had been compounded by the beating. He was a man for whom beating women came naturally, it was part of what he did with women; it was the only way he could let go completely. There were parties at his house where he dressed like a satyr and beat women with whips. He paid them to ask for more. Like a little dog who takes hold of the female with his teeth and shakes and shakes her in between coming.

However it was, he didn't mean to have a dying woman on his hands, and suddenly he did. That's when he was fully conscious of the harm he'd done and he chose it again and again. Each minute he waited to get help for her, he was choosing to let her die.

How do I know all this?

When we were in our thirties, my lover married someone else, and I painted my apartment red. Not a rust color or a burgundy, this was the most fake food dye maraschino red that I could find. I painted it myself, spread the bright stain over the light switches, the vents, the electrical outlets, even the ceiling.

Only six months after his wedding, my lover started coming by again. I was a woman he would sleep with but not one he would marry. It hadn't of course seemed that way to me. It was the 1920s. I loved him.

It was different after. Sometimes we made love when I was bleeding. He would turn me over on my belly where we couldn't see each others' faces. I heard him groan, he could

watch it all and he felt, he said, like an animal. You could
forget you were human, he said, the blood, it was so good to
watch. You see? What a relief it was to him, this man who
thought too much. Face down on the bed, I would tilt my
head and look for a mirror where I could catch a glimpse of
his face. All I saw was red. He took a shower before he went
back home to his wife; there was blood underneath his nails,
smears of it on his thighs and arms. How could he have explained it? When he left, I made a smear over the red paint,
and at first it blended in but in the morning there was a
brownish stain.

I felt shame then, actually, and I couldn't wait for him to
call the next day, to reassure me that he'd loved it. Me. Had I
loved it? I'm a strong woman in most areas of my life, but it
occurs to me now that I didn't ask myself that question. I
asked myself very few questions when it came to him. I loved
that he loved it. I'm ashamed of that as well. Or not ashamed.
If I had it to do over, I'd do it the same way.

The red walls of my apartment would glow in the afternoon sun like the inside of a heart. The rhythm of his life
brought him to that apartment over and over again. You see?
The rhythm of *his* life.

I've been obsessed for years with what kind of hat it
was. I wish the jurors had asked to see it, I wish I'd looked
in Madge's closet. It didn't occur to me until the middle of
the trial that it was the key to knowing why and how
things happened. A large hat, veiled, would have meant
something different than a straw hat with fruit. Was she still a
woman with enough sense of a self that would continue to
live and need a hat, or was she a woman who wanted to
cover the bruises just long enough to buy the poison that
would kill her?

Or maybe there was the tiniest bit of hope, and when the hat didn't do its work, that was the end of it.

Whatever hat it was, I feel like Madge has sent the memory of it spinning through the years to me, to any woman who would hear this story, and if I could only see it clearly, only latch onto the meaning of it, I would know how to get through my own grief, my own anger. She was a young woman then and had no idea what she was doing, but it was a gift somehow, her purchase of that hat. I would have read that hat for days to find its meaning. If it was the right hat, I thought, it would give me the courage I needed, a kind of hat I could use to demand things or to whisk him out the door.

In the end, Steve went to prison for his crime. Though it was clear from the trial that no one really cared about Madge. At that point he had become simply an embarrassment to everyone, even the Klan, and they had to get rid of him. In that sense, Madge was a martyr.

You know how, during the plague, they locked up the house when someone in the family became infected? And even after the infection was in the house, the people would do anything they could to escape that confinement, so there were guards at the doors who had to steel themselves to the screaming, the bribes, the tricks of those trapped inside? I'm not sure why I'm bringing this up, I'm old, but somehow I think that what they wanted to escape was not the house, but the disease, even after it was within them. There's always some disease we're trying to escape, and the night train is easy transportation. In my lover's case, it was the house of his body, its limits. He was desperately afraid of dying. In my case, it was the closed-in house of what I knew. I wanted mystery. And maybe in the end that was true of Madge as well.

A trial is just an attempt to make a story out of the facts. Both sides wedge their stories into the cracks in the other one, like scientific theories, like religion, like any stories. But maybe in the end the night train never makes sense in the light of day. It roars through the orderly towns and farms and graveyards and breaks them up like children's toys. We all wear masks at night. Maybe hers was a large-brimmed hat to cover the face that seemed unmasked and fragile in the light. Which face was the real one? Me, I rode that train for most of my adult life, no brakes on, the wind so harsh through the open windows. I rode the train and at the same time never left that room. Who am I now? There were Stephensons coming to power then all over Europe. Madge and I standing beside each other in our college yearbook. So innocent, we thought, so trusting. Hearts open, hands clutching the fare.